CRADLE SONG

Also by Jane Rawlinson:

THE LION AND THE LIZARD

CRADLE SONG

JANE RAWLINSON

St. Martin's Press
New York

Library of Congress Cataloging in Publication Data

Rawlinson, Jane.
Cradle song.

I. Title.
PR6068.A924C7 1986 823'.914 86-13790
ISBN 0-312-17075-0

First published in Great Britain by André Deutsch Limited.

First U.S. Edition

10 9 8 7 6 5 4 3 3 2 1

CRADLE SONG

CHAPTER 1

Everything was ready for the birth. The white room gleamed. The midwife's apron crackled in the corridor. Ayah, who was fifteen and came from the local village, watched and waited.

Ursula had stood in the yard, her hands resting on the shelf of stomach that was her baby, while Ayah was scrubbed under the cold tap with delousing shampoo. Then all the other servants took their turn since one could never be too careful. Ursula had read from cover to cover the book on tropical hygiene presented to her by George on their engagement three years earlier.

In most matters, Ursula still relied on her own judgement. There was a sturdiness about Ayah that Ursula believed augured well for reliability though the midwife in her professional capacity considered another possible cause for her shape. The midwife decided it was none of her business and that the memsahib should not be worried at such a time.

Ayah dusted the dustless room under supervision. She mopped the clean floor with just a touch of disinfectant in the water. Foreign germs were somehow so much more threatening than British germs.

'Now take all the clothes out of the cupboard and wash them,' said the midwife.

Ayah was puzzled. No baby had ever worn the tiny vests or crumpled the sheets but then perhaps white babies were different. She had never seen one before so this was perhaps quite normal.

How white the sun bleached the miniature garments! If possible they were even whiter than before. Ayah smiled as she squinted at the washing line. She smiled as she folded the nightdresses warm and smelling of sunshine, as she ironed out every crinkle and crevice.

Ayah put down the iron to pick her nose and wipe her finger on the apron that should be spotless. She sang as she worked when she thought no one was listening. She polished the pram and glowed at the thought of days strolling under the acacias, wheeling the baby to and fro under the eyes of her lover, the gardener.

On her hands and knees, Ayah peered at Memsahib through the spokes. Memsahib, who rarely smiled, heaved herself up from her chair by means of the verandah railings. She lurched down the steps and waddled into the garden.

Ayah giggled, a glint of white teeth in the chrome hub cap. Memsahib looked so funny.

'Of course you imagined the cloud,' said George.

That was typical of him, thought Ursula. He had woken late. Breakfast was late and he was annoyed because his usual routine was disturbed by the meeting of farmers in Kitale at midday.

But there was a cloud, no bigger than a man's hand. It hovered on the horizon while Ursula watched, Ursula and the animals of the plains, transfixed in a limbo of hope. They endured the cracked earth, the spiked shade in the knowledge of what was to come.

Ursula had often marvelled over the ability of the impala to withhold giving birth until the time was right. Until green spears pierced the earth's softened crust and thrust their way towards light and warmth.

'The rains are weeks off yet,' said George, but he didn't see the cloud any more than he saw the moon set or the dawn break, or the movement of gaunt animals through a sunrise which set the world on fire.

Ursula was glad when George had gone out. She thought she was in labour and wanted to be alone. She had felt only a few twinges, the first stirrings of her cervical muscles. She walked across the lawn conscious of her servants' eyes which followed every move, determined not to waddle in spite of the pressure of the child's head between her legs.

Not that she would have called the area in front of the house a lawn any more. It had become a desolate wasteland surrounded by cracked and fissured soil that was once flowerbed. Burnt umber, thought Ursula, described perfectly the effect of months of searing sunshine and incompetent gardening. She sometimes wondered why she bothered to employ a gardener. For a native, who ought to be used to the heat, his work and achievements were remarkably few.

It gave Ursula pleasure to see the house from a distance. Three years ago the building stood in isolation amid a clearing at the foot of the escarpment. Now its outline was softened by flowering shrubs whose deep roots withstood heat and drought. For the future, Ursula had visions of a real garden with green lawns, shady trees and a lake at whose edge her son would run naked, a flash of white against the dark waters.

She was certain that her child was a son. Already she loved him passionately, her son and the picture of herself as her son's mother. She only feared losing the perfect relationship which she now had with the child in her womb, mother and child in a perfect communion which admitted no other person.

Ursula had moved into the small white nursery she had created, so that she might be alone with her dreams. The excuse she gave to George was rather different. She disturbed him often during the night, troubled by cramp and the tattoo of her son's fists against her bladder.

'It's my child too. I want to be disturbed,' said George.

Ursula had laughed and replied that George's sleep was of paramount importance. And George had mocked Ursula's conviction that the baby was a son.

'There's a fifty fifty chance you're right,' he said as if life depended on the toss of a coin. But Ursula knew. She had become more certain month by month as the child grew. A mother knew these things.

Ursula thought more of her own mother during these days of waiting, though they had never been close. Her mother produced short quotations suited to every occasion. 'In pain and sorrow shalt thou bring forth children' was one of her favourites, coupled with a slight tightening of the lips and a certain grim satisfaction.

Ursula's mother! Passiontide services with knees ridged and blue on the wooden kneelers. Now Ursula longed for her mother's disapproval. She crouched foetus-like, arms wrapped around her legs, forehead pressed against the flat plate of her knee caps, bowed under the leaden weight of pain.

Before her eyes small things were suddenly very clear. Ursula saw as if for the first time the tiny trails of ants through the dust and a small white pebble glinting in the sun.

'You shouldn't be here on your own.' The midwife's voice jarred through the birdsong.

'Take your time dear,' she said, relieved there was already something to do since first babies were so unreliable. There was no rush. She had come to stay for a month and the country made a welcome break from Nairobi. If it took all morning to get her patient back to the house, what did it matter? The sun was hot, the view pleasant. If dinner last night was anything to go by, lunch would be excellent. Her room was comfortable, the servants were polite and efficient.

The two women stopped to watch a bee-eater swoop and vanish into its nest in the bank. Ursula had not bothered with a hat. The sun scorched a red line down the centre of her head along the parting. Sweat trickled down her forehead and her dress clung wet under her arms.

The gardener stared from his vantage point in the shade of a jacaranda. He was almost invisible, his skin one with the shadows and the rich dark soil. He had no name but that of his place of work, Shamba, meaning Garden. In rank he was placed below the other servants since his job was unskilled and made him dirty. He also performed the tasks inside the house which the servants refused to do.

To Ayah, a recent arrival from her village, he was tall and slim and beautiful. She had never seen anyone like him before.

Shamba had weeded in the sun until the earth swam before his eyes. Miracles were worked through his two gardening tools. One panga, shaped like a scimitar, trimmed bushes, lopped trees, cleared drains and uprooted trees. It was knife, axe, saw, fork, spade and secateurs in one. The other panga, long and slim, tapered and curved at the tip, was for grass cutting.

Shamba noticed Memsahib was sweating and as stooped as his own mother. He also kept an eye on the washing line. He had hidden one fragile nightdress in the jungle of passion-flower creeper which screened the nearby septic tank.

'Soon Ayah, she come look,' he thought.

Through the nursery window Ayah watched Memsahib move slowly up the verandah steps. She stopped on each stair, gripping the banisters for support.

'I help Memsahib?' wondered Ayah, but did not dare to touch Memsahib's skin with her black hand. Ayah arranged the baby clothes in a neat pile, warm from the sun and the iron. She counted once. She counted twice. A nightgown was missing and her heart stood still.

She wondered whether she could make her way unseen to the washing line, through the back door and under cover of the passion flower.

Shamba saw her leave the house, and smiled.

Preparations for lunch were underway in the kitchen. Simeon planned on a lavish scale for the two white ladies. There would be avocado pear from the garden followed by . . .

'What we have Charity, soufflé or quiche?'

Charity shrugged and couldn't decide. She liked both.

'We have quiche. Soufflé soon go flop.' Simeon gestured eloquently with his hands and reflected that planning leftovers was also an art. He removed the homemade rolls from the oven and sent Charity to gather lettuce, tomatoes and radishes. To round off the meal he sliced pineapple and pawpaw.

'Memsahib not each lunch,' announced Charity after peeping through the french windows onto the verandah.

♦

Ursula's contractions had become more frequent and stronger. Her cervix was almost fully dilated. She was nearing the end of the first stage of labour. Her hands on the arms of her chair were at intervals quite white. Between contractions she relaxed and dozed until Shamba returned from the passion-flower creeper to sharpen his panga on the edges of the stone path beneath the verandah.

It was not just the noise that irritated Ursula, nor the time spent in this occupation, but the fact that he actually wore the metal away. The metal became thinner and more brittle and finally snapped at the rate of one new ten-shilling panga every six months. And the lawn still looked terrible. It was cut twice as often in the shade of the trees by the river as anywhere else. In the long intervals unbroken by the hiss and swish of the blade, Ursula suspected Shamba sat on the back doorstep drinking tea. Her tea.

On the floor at Ursula's feet lay a large black slug. It had crawled from the vegetation surrounding the verandah during the night and had, for some reason, remained. Perhaps injured by a broom or passing foot, it was still alive, writhing as ants tore away its flesh. By the time Ursula rose from her chair, unable to bear her pain alone any longer, the slug had disappeared as if it had never existed.

Ursula stood, unable to move and called out in fear. The midwife walked slowly along the verandah and took Ursula in her arms like a child.

The servants listened intently and shook their heads. Charity reset the table for one. Simeon scraped half the food off the tray onto two plates for himself and Charity.

'Is better we eat it hot,' he said and seated himself at the kitchen table.

Water poured down Ursula's legs and gathered in a pool on the floor. She froze with disgust. Ayah giggled and ran for a cloth. She mopped up and wrung the water over the verandah railings. She watched the splattered patterns on the dusty leaves and heard the foliage rattle. She mopped and squeezed again. So much water!

◆

Ursula lay in the small white room where the curtains moved as gently as in a dream. It was cool there, where the wide overhang of the eaves kept out the sun. She lay as white as marble, chiselled from the same whiteness as the sheets. She had lifted her long, dark hair from beneath her neck to spread upwards in a fan over the pillow. She always slept with her hair brushed in this way. It was cool, and she had once held up a mirror and been pleased with the effect, like that of a mermaid with heavy hair suspended in the water.

Ursula lay immobile, her features composed. She allowed others to see only what she wanted them to see of herself. Cold, she had been called, but that, she knew, was because they did not know her. They saw only the features that would not have disgraced a Grecian statue, the smooth brow, a face that could have been beautiful had it ever been animated. But Ursula believed that displays of emotion were vulgar.

As if she were two people, Ursula was aware at the same time, of her pain, and of life carried on as usual in the outside world. Shamba sang and grated his panga on the stone path. Up and down, up and down the metal screamed.

'Go away,' shouted the nurse through the open window, waving her arms dark against the brightness.

The nursery was simple, with unpainted furniture and white walls. A jug of bougainvillea provided the only splash of colour. There were one or two religious pictures and an ebony crucifix which gave the room the contrived simplicity of a nun's cell.

Ursula had enjoyed the convent whose large, dark door swung shut on the world and her father's death. Life calmly and predictably followed the church calendar in a relentless cycle of joy and sorrow, love and suffering.

The Stations of the Cross offered the challenge of turning through three hundred and sixty degrees perched on a kneeler, through all the appropriate psalms and genuflections without holding onto the back of the pew. The Polish sisters who spoke no English knelt amid a cracking of knee joints and the girls grinned under their black veils.

Bubbles of memory floated on the surface of Ursula's mind. Robes fluttered woodenly in the wind of childhood. Thoughts drifted as serene and gentle as the face whose body bore the weight of the cross while his body twisted in torment.

Behind the altar had been an Italian triptych, Mother and Child on a background of gold leaf, illuminated by mutual love. There they were every morning frozen in a warm eternity that brought tears to Ursula's eyes, and a yearning to know such love herself.

Such devotion brought an invitation to tea, with cakes and hot buttered toast and Reverend Mother. There she sat by the Adam fireplace, a gaunt smile cracking her face and her wimple creaking. A Polish sister brought with the tea tray a smell of boiled potatoes and hot fat.

'Milk or lemon, Ursula?' inquired Reverend Mother and dabbed her upper lip with a lace-trimmed handkerchief.

'Lemon please, Reverend Mother.' Ursula had never had tea with lemon before but it sounded grown-up.

'Sugar?'

'No thank you, Reverend Mother.' Ursula was proud of her unworldly image. She doubted whether an aesthete would have a sweet tooth. She watched aghast as the nun plopped three sugar lumps into her own cup, and tried not to screw up her face as she sipped her own.

'My child,' began Reverend Mother, 'we have witnessed your great devotion to our Blessed Lord (bowed head, sign of the cross.) Has it ever occurred to you that you may have a vocation?'

Ursula could only sit and reflect dumbly that she could tell her friends she had seen a nun drinking. With her wimple on.

'Yes, my child. It is not everyone who is called, but it would be a grave sin to resist His bidding.'

Ursula imagined a vocation like a huge dark shape pursuing her along dim corridors at night. She could almost feel its hands around her throat.

Ursula never doubted that she had a vocation, though not in the direction foreseen by Reverend Mother. Her sense of dedication to some higher ideal did not include God or self-sacrifice. Nor did it include men, for since her father's death there had been no male presence in her life.

Ursula saw the priest, the doctor and her mother's lawyer. She read Jane Austen and saw that the highest ideal in manhood was a somewhat nebulous figure whose greatest happiness was achieved in being allowed to pander to the woman he loved.

And what was love? Ursula read her schoolbooks, the New Testament, the psalms and pre-Raphaelite poetry. Love, she equated with worship of an ideal being. Man worshipped woman, a woman worshipped her child. Ursula longed for a child to love.

The threat of a vocation soon ceased to trouble Ursula. Before her eyes remained the inspiration of Mary the mother, who produced a glowing child, a son who would glorify his mother and bring her eternal joy and love. But first came the sorrow.

I will lift mine eyes unto the mountains. Cragged snow-capped peaks cool and glacial. Crisp crust of virgin snow. Frosted drifts deep in childhood, curling and breaking, foaming over hidden blue caverns. The froth of piped icing, birthdays, weddings, christenings. The crackle and crunch of wimples and aprons.

But not this. Calvary is not for me. The leaves of my missal, transparent, fluttering golden like butterflies and fingers too clumsy to turn the pages. Take this chalice from me. A woman steps forward and wipes my face. One moment of compassion. A tepid sponge to dull the salt-lash of sweat.

How could I know when I chose this path? And we have been so happy, my son and I. Yea, though I should walk through the valley of the shadow of evil, he comforts me.

At the ninth hour a darkness fell over all the land. With a great cry he yielded up his spirit. The dark skull between my legs wet with the waters of the womb and eyes screwed tight against the blinding light.

I feel the pain of air invading his lungs, the bed linen like sackcloth for He who has walked on water. My heart stops at the thin wail of terror. 'Come to me all ye who labour and are weary. Trust me. I will bear your pain.'

♦

The child's cry was heard with satisfaction in the corridor and through the open window, where Shamba crouched weeding silently in the cool of the late afternoon.

CHAPTER 2

The nurse gave Ayah lessons in baby care. There was so much to learn, so much equipment involved for one small being who occupied in volume perhaps one cubic foot of air.

'Whatever you do with Baby, you must first wash your hands.'

Ayah trotted over to the washbasin. It was wonderful this water in abundance. She put in the plug and turned on the taps which gleamed, reflecting her distorted image – Ayah with a long thin face and short distended body – while the water sparkled against the white china.

Ayah laughed and lowered her hands into the warm water, so black against the white. She rubbed the soap between her palms until it foamed and bubbled and her skin was as slippery as that of a newborn baby. Backwards and forwards, backwards and forwards, her hands drifted limply through dancing diamonds of light and water. Out came the plug and Ayah wiped her hands on the towel (clean each day). She watched three pints of precious water gurgle their way down the drain towards the septic tank.

Ayah's mother walked two miles to the river for water. The rains were late and the village well had run dry. She carried the water home on her head in a large gourd and rationed every drop. She washed herself and her children in the turgid brown current stirred by the feet of hippo and elephant. She went in company with the other women, who laughed and talked and sang as they walked and washed.

Ursula enjoyed her shower. She rinsed away the sweat of the previous day and felt refreshed in her yellow bath cap trimmed with lace. Charity often wore this when she cleaned the bathroom and she studied her reflection in the glass and tiles while she worked.

Ursula liked her shower to be at precisely body temperature so that it felt neither hot nor cold. The water fell with a pleasant thrum onto her shoulders then trickled down her breasts and stomach.

She looked down and felt a sagging emptiness and yearned for yesterday. Yesterday had been so full of promise, her child leapt in her womb. Now there was nothing. She had been promised the earth and all she had received was a handful of dust.

George sat by the cradle overwhelmed with such love for his daughter that he felt close to tears. He would have liked to touch her but was inhibited by the presence of Ayah and the midwife. He sat and watched, impervious to the disapproval caused by his disruption of the nursery routine.

His feelings were similar to those he had experienced when he first brought his bride to the farm. He had already spent a few years in the country himself and had ceased to think of it as being very different from the East Anglian farm of his childhood. Through Ursula's eyes he was forced to see the wonder and strangeness of it all and it had made him feel immensely protective towards her.

But it was the hour for cleaning the floor. The midwife looked at the floor, at her watch, and at George's dusty boots and frowned. Instead there would be a lesson in bottle washing.

So Ayah washed bottles, ones that were already clean, for practice. It was wonderful, thought Ayah, the way such a wide brush squeezed through the narrow neck. She had to learn not to splash soap bubbles over the floor as the bristles popped out. A slippery floor might cause accidents.

Ayah put one sterilising tablet in the transparent container and watched as it spat and shrank and finally vanished. The bottles were slippery from the soapy water and one slid through her fingers onto the floor while Ayah gasped and pressed her hands against her head. The bottle landed safely on the carpet.

'Now you will have to wash it again,' said the midwife.

Ayah was puzzled.

'Memsahib, please, what these bottles are for?'

The midwife was startled, it all went to prove one of the theories she had about locals. She snorted and decided the question did not merit an answer. But George looked up and smiled at the girl.

'They are for feeding the little memsahib. You put a piece of rubber here, and the baby sucks.' He put the teat into his own mouth by way of demonstration. The midwife frowned and Ayah clapped her hands and laughed. Then she put her hand over her mouth, very serious all of a sudden.

'Memsahib, she sick?'

Memsahib was not sick though she wondered what all the fuss was about. From a shady corner of the verandah she watched George and Ayah cuddle and fuss over her daughter. She felt that nobody understood, though she stood like the statue of Jesus in the school chapel, with cloak parted to expose her raw and bleeding heart.

'Except perhaps the nurse,' thought Ursula.

'Don't worry dear,' said the midwife, 'a lot of mothers don't take to their first. It takes time.'

'Post-natal depression,' said Bill. He lived some twenty miles away as the crow flies and was their nearest European neighbour. And Bill ought to know, thought George, he had several children who never kept still for long enough to be counted. But what reason had Ursula to be depressed? George's concern knew no bounds. He almost stifled her with loving kindness, his Madonna, mother of his child.

'Would you like the light out?'

'Are you warm enough?'

'Shall I bring you a drink?'

'Would you like to go out today?'

'Shall I read to you?'

Ursula shrank further back into her corner and longed only to be left alone. She did not want to go out, she did not want to do anything, only to try and piece together the shattered fragments of her dreams.

There in front of her lay the garden, a retreat from the squalling, puking infant, the dirty nappies and Ayah's dreary singsong. She threw all her creative energy into its design. George supported every whim in the hope that it would do her good.

'A lake?' queried Muriel. Muriel was Bill's wife from across the valley, with tightly permed hair and a brood of children whom she insisted on looking after herself. She fussed and clucked constantly. Ursula found her continual anxiety about children wearisome.

'Yes,' replied Ursula. 'To follow the valley contours.'

'But what about the children?'

'There are always servants around.'

George placed a bench in the shelter of some hibiscus and poinsettia bushes at a place which overlooked the whole project. From her seat, the ground dropped steeply down towards the stream. She sat, constantly frustrated by the rate of progress. If she left her post to supervise Susan's feeds all activity ceased. So she remained in her chair from dawn to dusk and the water level rose inch by inch.

And inch by inch Susan grew, the pride and joy of her ayah. At night Ayah lay with her hands on her stomach and dreamed not of tiny, dark, fluttering limbs but of the baby with skin like fresh milk and hair the colour of ripe maize, and longed for the morning to come.

Behind the house a spring bubbled from the cliff-face of the Mau Escarpment, and flowed through the pipes of the house, the length of the garden and beyond into the arid plains. While the lake filled, George was forced to water his cattle by cart. Further away a whole village was on the move, fathers, mothers, goats, sheep, cattle and children. The village was burnt and the people moved on, for water meant life. And still the water level rose in the lake until Ursula could see her own reflection.

Ursula sat and her dreams were of deep dark pools, the heavy grey green of reflected foliage. She dreamt of a child at the water's edge whose white limbs threshed the surface, weightless as in the waters of the womb.

'What about mosquitoes?' asked George.

Ursula, after consultation with the health authority, introduced carp into the lake. It was perhaps a needless precaution with the main body of the water gently flowing, but there were still backwaters and it was as well to be sure.

She worried that the servants failed to take even the most basic preventive measures. In her house the beds were securely netted but though she provided the house servants with nets they ruined them within days.

At dusk, Ursula ordered that the house windows should be closed before any lights were turned on. The servants were spared that trouble because their rooms had no windows, but they didn't even bother to close the doors.

'What more can I do?' wondered Ursula. She and George tried to calculate the number of working days lost due to malaria. The figure was astronomical.

Shamba shared Ayah's single bed, provided by Memsahib. Ayah loved the way the luminous pink net transformed her whole room when she lay in bed and looked through it. But the bed was cheap, the metal springs sagged beneath the weight of two people and snagged the net where it was tucked underneath the mattress.

On the first morning, Ayah awoke horrified by the gashes in her rose-coloured spectacles. While Memsahib ate her breakfast Ayah crept to her room with a needle and thread from her employer's workbox.

On the second morning more repairs were needed. This time Ayah bolted the door while she sewed the jagged edges together. On the third morning she put off her mending until evening. On the fourth, she merely shrugged. By the time the net was a week old the holes would have allowed an elephant to pass through. Ayah took down the net and stuffed it under her bed.

In Ayah's home village there was no malaria, only drought. The mosquito could not breed at this time of year. The cattle and sheep gave no milk, nor did the women.

CHAPTER 3

The rains came and Ursula's garden grew. Busy Lizzie rampaged under the trees beside the lake, glowing like a carpet of orange stars in the semi-darkness.

Ayah dreamt that Susan was her baby. She often touched the porcelain skin and trailed her fingers through the downy hair. She prepared Susan's feeds entirely on her own, washed nappies, cleaned the nursery every day and rinsed the little garments with joy.

When the work was done Ayah put Susan in the pram and strolled down the garden. Shamba whistled and beckoned but she ignored him. She had Susan to consider and she was becoming uncomfortably large for a roll in the bushes. The middle button at the centre front of her uniform was a good inch apart from its mate, the centre buttonhole. Luckily a snow-white apron with bib could hide a multitude of sins.

Ursula, sewing on the verandah, happened to glance down the garden. Something about Ayah's rolling gait struck a chord of sympathy but counted-thread work demanded a good deal of concentration. She banished the half-formed thought from her mind. She did not even look up when Charity brought a tray of tea and some newly baked scones.

'Memsahib, please. I go home early. My father, she die.'

'He,' corrected Ursula. Only a few stitches remained to

complete the outside border. One thread out in any direction would mean hours of unpicking, so much wasted time. Charity hovered, and cast a shadow on the white linen.

'I thought your father died last month.'

'No, Memsahib. That was brother of my father.'

'You told me it was your father.'

'Is same thing, Memsahib.'

Ursula wondered how it could be the same thing but to say Charity could not go when there was the slightest element of doubt worried her. And it was Simeon's half day, the servants were so inconsiderate.

'Has Simeon left any dinner?'

'Yes, Memsahib. She leave cold meat and salad.'

'He,' corrected Ursula. Charity started undoing her apron and bolted across the verandah with a broad smile on her face.

Memsahib did not look up to see the smile, nor did she see that Ayah was not pushing the pram along by its handle so much as using it to drag herself along.

Evening approached and night fell like a curtain. The silken blackness was heavy with a chorus of crickets and the harsh croaking roar of bull frogs.

Ayah took more time than usual over putting Susan to bed. She knelt on the floor next to the blue plastic bath and cupped water in her hand to pour over the soapy body. She shook a snowfall of powder onto her dark pink palm to smooth under Susan's arms and among the folds under her chin. She held the child naked on her knee and smoothed the golden hair with a soft brush.

While the kettle boiled for ten minutes to destroy all possible germs Ayah arranged a bib of embroidered Swiss cotton over the white nightgown. The room filled with steam. At last Susan's bottle stood in a jug of cold water to cool.

Susan smacked her lips over tiny spoonfuls of scraped avocado pear.

'Is good baby?' asked Ayah. Susan smiled and green slime trickled down her chin onto the bib. Down went the bottle of milk and up came the wind. Ayah arranged a muslin nappy over her shoulder and walked along the verandah, singing quietly and patting Susan's back.

Ursula looked up as the footsteps and song stopped next to her. She lowered her sewing and held out her arms. Ayah put Susan on her mother's knee where she was held, at arm's length.

Ursula inquired after Susan's diet and bowels. Susan was restless and uncomfortable held in a sitting position with her stomach gorged. She brought up most of the avocado and milk in a delicate mossy-green jet over her mother's skirt. Then she smiled sweetly. Ayah laughed and clapped her hands.

'Bed time,' said Ursula and retired to change.

Ayah stumbled as she turned to go. Ursula made a mental note to check on the drinks cabinet before dinner, for her daughter's sake.

Susan's eyelids drooped and closed on her ayah's shoulder to the sound of an ancient two-tone lullaby.

'Lul—la, Susan la,' murmured Ayah. She lowered the baby into the sterile cot, enveloped in frilled layers of white netting like a bride.

That evening, the house was very quiet. While Ayah and Shamba had the servants' yard to themselves, George and Ursula remarked how pleasant it was to enjoy the privacy of their own home.

They sprayed themselves liberally with insect repellent and carried the tray of prepared food onto the verandah. They ate in silence as they were used to do in the dining room in front of Charity, with Simeon eavesdropping from the kitchen.

Then George opened a bottle of wine by way of celebration. Ursula inquired about the farm and how the cattle were coping with the heat. George inquired after Ursula's garden and hoped the plants were not suffering. Ursula wondered whether now would be a good time to broach the subject of a lawn-mower, and George, who had arrived after Ayah had left, would have liked to hear every minute detail about Susan's day.

Ursula stacked the plates and George carried them out to the scullery. He returned with the lemon mousse and poured more wine. The novelty of the situation struck him, the air of a midnight feast in the dorm.

'Did I ever tell you . . .?' he began and Ursula resigned herself to a series of adventures set in an average boys' boarding school in the south of England. She wondered whether George had ever really grown up. The mousse was too sweet but she tried to laugh in the appropriate places. It made a change from the farm talk.

George was still talking half an hour later when quite unexpectedly the face of Shamba loomed out of the darkness, his eyes gleaming in the lamplight.

'Memsahib, please, come quick. My wife.'

'We are eating,' replied Ursula, spooning on.

'Oh yes, Memsahib. Sorry, Memsahib. Please you come.'

They established that though the matter would not wait until morning it was not so urgent that Memsahib was required to abandon her lemon mousse.

'I didn't even know he had a wife,' said Ursula.

'Did you know that if black people closed their eyes you wouldn't be able to see them in the dark?' George remarked.

Ursula giggled. The evening was becoming very silly.

'I expect it's malaria.' She took a bottle of quinine from the medicine cupboard and set off.

The servants' quarters always put her in a bad mood. She had tried nagging, fines, and docking wages. The only result had been rebellion and resignations. So she tried to avoid the area which upset her, and pushed it to the back of her mind. There were occasions like now when she was called upon to perform the role of ministering angel.

Ursula turned on the outside light and stepped onto the back doorstep. She passed the dustbins on her left and the woodpile on her right before she left the circle of electric light. She switched on her torch and continued up the concrete steps beyond the garage and the tool-shed, into the walled yard in front of the servants' quarters.

Ursula picked her way carefully through litter and chicken droppings towards the line of rooms, each with a door opening into the yard. There were no windows on that side which would have looked directly onto the back door. Besides, everyone knew that the servants disliked windows since glass was easily broken, turning windows into doors. The servants didn't trust each other.

Unwashed pans clonked against Ursula's ankles and washing clung to her hair. She shone the torch beam along the closed doors, one, two, three, and made her way towards the fourth which stood slightly ajar, showing a glimmer of light.

'Where is your wife?' she asked.

Shamba looked up from the floor. He leant against the bed rolling a ball of sticky grey maize meal between his fingers. With his head he indicated the direction Ursula should take though he did not move himself.

Ursula trod warily round the back of the building towards the latrines. The floor was of earth, the cracked china bowls set into the ground were clogged with excrement and newspaper. Since the cisterns were always in need of repair, it was Shamba's job to carry buckets of water and flush the pans night and morning. Otherwise the flies might carry a danger of dysentery into Memsahib's kitchen. But it was not a pleasant job.

Amid the garbage squatted Shamba's wife, with a paraffin lamp next to her. Ursula looked down on the slender neck, the bowed head with hair drawn tightly into tiny plaits, one in the centre of each circle, the size of a penny.

'Why are you not in bed?' asked Ursula, meaning, why should she be summoned to this stinking place.

The girl looked up briefly before her eyes closed again. She gave a deep grunting moan. Ursula recognised vaguely that the cotton dress pulled up around the girl's waist had once belonged to her. There was something familiar about the face, the broad nose, the wide mouth.

'Ayah?' asked Ursula.

George wondered what could be keeping his wife for so long. He carried out the thermos of coffee and sipped alone with his feet up on the verandah railing. He inhaled the perfume of the moonflower-vine and sighed. He hoped Ursula would return soon, perhaps they would go to bed early, together for once.

♦

Shamba finished his posho and hurried outside. His pace quickened when he heard Memsahib call. As George said, it was very easy for a black man to become invisible in the darkness.

Ursula returned to kneel on the dirt floor. She saw the baby's head a darker shadow between its mother's legs, advance and recede with each contraction like sodden driftwood caught in the tide's edge.

'Why me?' she wondered. 'Why did they call me? Why can't they cope on their own? It must be quite natural for them.'

She knelt and waited, sitting back on her heels to ease the pressure on her knees. She was soon attacked by the agonising cramp which afflicts people whose custom it is to sit on chairs and eat heavily salted food.

Ursula worried about the next morning. Who would give Susan her early morning feed? Who would push the pram? Who would wash the tiny clothes and clean the nursery? Who would change Susan's nappy, sing her songs and cuddle her? Who in short, would be Susan's mother tomorrow?

Ayah had no worries beyond ridding herself of the alien creature within her body. Ursula feared that the baby might be stuck. She should not have come, or George should have driven the girl to the nearest doctor. Shamba should have summoned a local midwife, anything rather than rest the responsibility on her.

The baby's head appeared, a black oval that grew and grew. The skin of the perinaeum stretched to breaking point then suddenly the head was out. Ursula edged forward and spread her skirt over the floor, over the mess. The baby slithered quickly from its mother. Ursula grabbed hold of one slimy ankle and arm.

'It's a boy,' said Ursula. She wrapped him in her skirt for the night air was cool and thought of the stable in Bethlehem with the stench of donkey and ox.

Ayah shivered as she squatted linked to her employer by the heavy length of umbilical cord. She longed for her mother to hold her in her arms and sing to her, for the joy and celebration in the whole village that would herald her son's birth but there was only this white woman holding her son who bleated like a newborn lamb.

Ursula, absorbed in the long dark lashes and tightly coiled hair, almost forgot Ayah. The body glowed darkly, the palms of his hands a deep rose as he gripped her finger.

The placenta was delivered, the cord cut and the two women parted. Ursula carried the baby to the house while her servant tidied up the mess.

For the first time Ursula bathed a baby. She felt the tiny limbs free from gravity float as soft and light as in the womb.

Susan whimpered in her sleep. Her cry rose to a shriek of despair. George took his feet off the verandah railing and hurried into the nursery.

Ursula laid the baby on a soft white towel on her knee. She dabbed spirit around the navel and sprinkled talcum powder on his tummy like frost on newly ploughed earth. She dressed the baby in white, in one of Susan's outgrown nightdresses, then wrapped him in a shawl.

Ursula held the baby close and inhaled his warm, sweet smell. The baby could be hers if she closed her eyes.

George came from the nursery into the kitchen with Susan over his shoulder. He met his wife coming from the other direction with a tiny head nestled black against her neck. He laughed at the contrast but wondered whether she hadn't overdone it, dressing the child up like that.

CHAPTER 4

Ursula lay in bed and worried, waiting for the sound of Susan waking up. She tried to remember what she usually had for breakfast. Was it cereal first, or fruit juice, or did they both follow in the middle of the morning, in which case the bottle came first?

She looked at George and knew that nothing would wake him. A day on the ranch mending fences yesterday, and rounding up all the cattle in preparation for a visit from the vet today, ensured that George slept soundly.

Susan began to stir. The sun rose, slanting through the trees. A breeze whispered through the leaves. Susan smiled and stretched her arms towards the dancing patterns of light and shade on the wall above her cot.

Shamba got up with a new swagger. He was the father of a son, a man of consequence. He was promoted from being his wife's lover to the position of Head of the Family. When Ayah brought his tea he accepted it solemnly, as befitted his new role.

Charity came to see the baby and laughed. 'Little Bwana' she called him in his fine white clothes. She was cheerful for one whose father had died on the previous day.

Susan kicked off her blankets. The morning air was chilly and soon she was cold. Pangs of hunger gnawed at her stomach. She cried for milk and warmth.

Ursula hurried to the nursery with fruit juice, straight from the fridge. She mixed the bland cereal and wondered how she would survive the day.

Susan roared and wriggled while her nappy was changed. Ursula looked with horror on the untidy, thrashing bundle that spat out fruit juice and screamed and choked on each mouthful of porridge.

At exactly seven o'clock Ayah arrived. She put on the kettle and took a bottle from the steriliser. She laughed at Memsahib's struggles and Memsahib stalked out of the nursery. Ayah looked as bright and cheerful as ever. She wore a clean uniform, now buttoned under her apron, and torn rags to catch the blood still draining from her womb.

By the time George and Ursula sat down to breakfast, peace had returned to the nursery. Ayah sat in the chair by the window on a large soft cushion. She cuddled Susan to her and the early morning sun beamed gently upon them as Susan drained her bottle.

Ayah's son lay on a heap of clothes on the floor of Shamba's room. His mother had locked the door to keep out the chickens. The child would come to no harm. His mother would call in on her way to the washing line. She would feed him during her tea breaks and at lunch time.

'Of course, she'll have to go,' said Ursula.

'Why?' asked George, from behind a farming magazine.

'I can't have that sort of thing going on in my house.'

'Why not?'

'Because it's disgusting, that's why not.'

'It seems perfectly natural to me.'

'But they're not married and she's too young.'

'She's old enough to look after Susan.'

'That's different. I'm here.'

'*Autre temps* . . .' George shrugged, buttering his toast.

'I have my daughter to consider.'

Charity came in with more toast. She had paused for a while in the corridor, listening. She would send a message for her sister to come at once. Simeon, from his post by the kitchen door, thought of a young girl in the village. She would be delighted to have Ayah's job and he would be delighted to have her share his room.

Two messengers were summoned, children of the farm labourers from their compound beyond the vegetable garden. Each was given a shilling and departed in utmost secrecy. Once out of sight of the house, they trotted along together.

Ayah sat in her chair in the sun oblivious of the machinations around her.

While Charity pegged out washing, Simeon seized the opportunity for a tête-à-tête with Memsahib.

'Memsahib is needing ayah? My sister she come help.'

When Simeon slipped out of the back door to gather herbs for a soufflé, Charity was there, whispering in Ursula's ear.

'Memsahib, please, I have sister. She very good girl. She need work. I tell her she come. She very good ayah.'

Ursula agreed to see the girls and was pleased that a change of ayah could be effected as easily as a change of clothing. She would speak to Ayah later when she had finished cutting out her new dress.

She pinned the pattern carefully to avoid waste, then couldn't find her scissors. She emptied her workbasket, certain they were there somewhere under the reels of cotton. She turned out a whole cupboard and rummaged through drawers. She called for Charity and Simeon.

'Where are my scissors?'

'Scissors, Memsahib?' they chorused, wide-eyed with innocence. Such lovely big, silver, shiny scissors.

'Where can they be, Memsahib?'

'You ask Ayah,' they suggested. 'You ask Shamba.'

'But I had them yesterday,' wailed Ursula.

'Is better you ask Shamba. Is bad man.' Charity had not forgotten his amorous pursuit of her before Ayah's arrival.

Ursula stormed down the garden. On her return, the scissors gleamed on top of George's desk.

'Look, Memsahib. Bwana she take,' smiled Ayah.

Ursula picked up the scissors and turned them over and over. She looked at Ayah, then at the scissors again, opening them wide and thought back to the scene in the latrines and the cutting of the cord.

Ayah stood with Susan over her shoulder, swaying from side to side and singing gently.

'You must go,' said Ursula.

'Go?' Ayah wrinkled her nose and shook her head.

'You find another job.'

'Job, Memsahib?'

'Yes, another job. You are a wicked girl. You take your baby and go.'

Ursula took some money from her pocket and held it out. Ayah stood still, her arms tightened around the baby.

'I not want money, I want stay with Susan.'

Ursula banged the money down impatiently on the table. She looked at her watch, picked up her scissors and snipped angrily. Such a wasted morning!

'You take your money, pack your bags and go. Now!'

She did not look up again. Ayah tucked Susan in her cot and went to her room. She wondered what all the fuss was about. Had the scissors upset Memsahib so much?

Simeon's sister arrived hot and panting and was brought into the presence of Memsahib with a mere hundred yards lead over her rival who was slightly plumper.

Charity scolded her sister for not running faster and sent her to her room. She would not speak to Simeon. The kitchen became the setting for a cold war. There was no talk and no laughter. Lines of demarcation were strictly observed. Simeon, keeper of the keys, became Memsahib's most loyal and devoted servant. It was not right, he said, to start on next week's tea and sugar rations. He and Charity drank their afternoon tea in silence, unsweetened, and made from Memsahib's refurbished breakfast tea leaves.

Charity refused to prepare the vegetables, that was a job for the cook. She left Simeon to wash his own aprons.

Ursula led Simeon's sister into the nursery. She was a beautiful child of about fourteen. Ursula wondered whether she should offer her a room in the house to protect her from Shamba. Then she decided that with her brother Simeon on the compound, the girl would be in no danger.

Simeon's sister had never been inside a house before. She followed Ursula in a daze and understood nothing of what she was told.

Ayah sat on her doorstep and watched Simeon's sister wheel the pram under the jacarandas. To see Shamba chat pleasantly to her usurper was no worse blow. She seemed to be replaceable in every respect.

Ursula continued her cutting out and congratulated herself. She had upheld her principles at no personal cost and by lunchtime she was tacking the bodice together.

To impress Memsahib with his skills in every respect,

Simeon cooked an unusually lavish lunch rich in cream and avocado. Ursula, who would have preferred a simple cheese sandwich but could not resist delicious dishes once they were in front of her, suffered from indigestion and had to lie down on her bed. She drew the curtains and knew that if she could only sleep for an hour, she would feel better.

Simeon read the instructions on the tin of milk powder and translated them to his protegée. The thought of exercising his droits de seigneur as head of the household filled him with delight.

The girl returned to the nursery and mixed the feed, but lumps of powder clogged the teat. The harder Susan sucked, the more wind she swallowed. She cried and struggled but still the milk would not flow. Simeon's sister asked Charity for advice. Charity shrugged and turned her back.

Ayah sat on her doorstep while the baby tugged at her breast. She heard Susan's cries and wept because she could not comfort her.

Ayah's replacement asked Simeon what to do. Simeon shook his head. He didn't know. He held the bottle up to the light and squinted at it. He saw the lumps and shook the bottle, as if it contained salad dressing, vigorously in both hands. Milk spurted out in a greasy fountain all over Ursula's newly cut-out dress.

At last Susan could drink, but the damage was done. In her distended stomach, the milk sat heavily on a large bubble of air. She pulled her knees up to her chin and writhed in pain. Simeon's sister cuddled and sang and jogged in vain. She paced up and down the verandah while the baby clawed at her shoulder and roared.

Ursula who had finally fallen asleep, rose in great wrath. She seized the screaming baby and shook her. As if the stopper had been removed from a well-shaken bottle of lemonade the tiny stomach disgorged its contents all down her mother's dressing gown. As she handed Susan back, Ursula caught sight of the grease-stained bodice of her new dress. Such lovely silk! She wondered if it would ever come off.

'Simeon,' she screamed. 'Get rid of this girl.'

♦

Charity paused in her dusting and smiled. She crept out of the back door and warned her sister to be ready at any time. She offered to wash Simeon's apron but he scowled and slammed the wash-house door in her face.

Ursula almost threw Susan into her cot, another door slammed. Ursula had a shower and two aspirins. The air became cooler towards evening and her temper subsided.

Dinner was late because Simeon was still sulking. Money (for procuring her the job) and sex done for in one blow! Through the kitchen window he glared at the figure of his erstwhile protegée slouching homeward through the trees. He creamed butter and sugar with unwonted vigour, never before were the egg whites so light.

'He is an excellent cook,' remarked George.

Ursula toyed with her passion-fruit soufflé. The cries from the bedroom had begun the moment she sat down to eat but the food was already served so the baby must wait.

Worn out from all the pain and crying earlier that afternoon Susan had not woken at her usual tea time. Ursula could have woken her but she was trying to sponge the stain off the silk and forgot the time.

Ayah sat with her own dark baby but her thoughts were on another child. Her bowl of posho lay next to her, uneaten. She couldn't eat. Susan was crying. Shamba was cross and had hit her. She wondered what she had done to make everyone angry with her. She had gone to work on time. Baby Susan had been happy and well.

Shamba was too upset to speak to Ayah. He blamed her for sending him for Memsahib last night. She could surely have managed on her own, there was nothing to it, women had babies every day. Memsahib need never have known about the child. She had not made any comment before about Ayah's shape. With two wages, they could easily have paid someone to care for the baby. A shilling a week would have been sufficient. It was one thing to be young and in love and rich, quite another to be head of a family on one wage and that the lower one.

♦

Ursula abandoned her dessert and later – plus baby and bottle – rejoined her husband on the verandah for coffee.

'I'll feed her,' George said and wondered when Susan would be old enough to enjoy a bedtime story.

Charity came to clear away the cups and brought her sister.

'This my sister, Memsahib. That girl, she no good. Simeon is bad man, Memsahib. That girl is not sister. My sister, she very good girl.'

The girl stared at her feet. She was heavy and awkward which Ursula decided would be an advantage since there would be no problems with the men servants.

On the first evening the girl broke one glass feeding bottle and got herself so entangled in Susan's mosquito net that it came loose from the ceiling. The intricacies of poppers and nappy pins seemed quite beyond her.

'Perhaps she's nervous,' said George, and Ursula hoped for better things in the morning.

Ayah slept by herself, locked in her bedroom by an irate Shamba. He had planned to share his bottle of beer with the other servants by way of celebration, instead, he drank alone.

Ayah thought of happy times in her room and of having to make way for Charity's sister in the morning. As Shamba would not let her stay she would have to go back to her mother, to hoe and harvest and carry water.

Simeon dreamt of Charity and of murder. He woke with his hands round the neck of his scrawny old wife Wambui and sighed.

Charity, anxious that her sister should do well, woke the poor child every few minutes with some new piece of advice. Her sister begged to be allowed to go home, back to her grandmother's to milk goats and gather firewood.

Ursula lay cold and rigid and decided that life had nothing more to offer her. She was angry with Ayah for causing such a disruption in her life, and she envied her, her warm dark son.

♦

Susan woke before dawn. Her feeding pattern of the day before had been disrupted, no one had remembered to give her her avocado pear for supper. She was hungry, her nappy was soiled and wet. Alone in the dark, she felt frightened.

Ursula padded disgruntled down the corridor, almost relieved that the day looked like fulfilling her worst expectations. After hours of tossing and turning she had at last sunk into a deep sweat-soaked sleep from which she fought to surface.

She put the kettle on to boil for tea and for Susan's bottle. She changed the nappy and left it with the one from the night before in a soggy heap under the washbasin.

The kettle boiled. Ursula drank her tea and felt comforted. Susan relaxed as the warm milk trickled down into her empty stomach. She lay quietly in her mother's arms and her eyes closed. But Ursula longed for her bed, to lose herself once more in sleep. She lowered Susan gently into the cot, inch by inch over the drop-side. Susan slept on until her body touched the cold sheets. Then she stiffened in protest and began to scream. She screamed for the soft curve and heart-beat of her ayah's breast, for the smell of sweat and dark skin and the comforting drone of the familiar lullaby.

Ursula stood and watched Susan scream, not knowing what to do, hating the child.

Ayah too wept for what she had lost. She wept for her dream world, the small white room filled with sunshine, and her white baby.

Her son was restless on the second night of his expulsion from the warm dark confines of the womb. He sucked and whimpered and demanded his mother knew not what. She was fifteen, alone and friendless, locked in a windowless room. She was thirsty and her head hurt where Shamba had hit her. Between her legs was a heavy, dragging ache. She wept quietly, without hope, fearful of waking Shamba who was asleep on the other side of the partition wall.

♦

Ursula drew the covers over Susan and tucked them in firmly then hurried from the nursery shutting the door behind her. The child was spoilt, she decided, she had had her own way too much. The next ayah must be stricter. She crawled back into bed and flattened herself against her husband's back, seeking warmth.

George misinterpreted the move. He pulled up her night-dress and rolled on top of her. Ursula tried to push him away, then gave up and lay back. She foresaw only the endless drudgery of days to come and resigned herself to the situation. She quite liked the idea of herself as a martyr.

Shamba released his son and his son's mother from their prison on his way to work. He turned the key and kicked the door open viciously. His head ached and the bright light hurt his eyes. Fortunately the child no longer lay on the ground but on his mother's knee as she cowered in a back corner of the room.

As soon as he had gone Ayah ran into the toilet. Here she bumped into Charity.

'You go soon,' said Charity. 'My sister, she need room.'

Shamba's door was padlocked. Ayah saw him walking down the garden with his pangas and decided she had better go to her mother's.

'You have cup tea?' offered Simeon, her ally in misfortune.

'You stay. You sleep in my bed.' He had never had a chance before, not with Shamba around.

'You want I send Wambui home?' asked Simeon. Wambui was his senior wife. He would even do that for Ayah.

Ayah turned away, too weary to think. But she had no intention of accepting Simeon's offer. He was such a big, old man and from another tribe.

Ayah fed her baby and sipped her tea. Then she stripped off the little boy's white gown and vest to return them to Memsahib.

Charity's sister clumped heavy footed down the corridor. She knocked a plant off the window sill as she went by and the pot shattered, scattering earth over the parquet floor. Ursula was awoken by the crash. Her head ached and she wondered whether she was ill or just short of sleep. George shot out of bed and saw how late it was. On his way to the bathroom he trod on a lump of soil and swore.

Charity's sister, on her hands and knees, tried to scrape the mess into her apron. She was so short-sighted that she had to feel around for the broken pieces of pot that she couldn't see.

'You go in nursery and you sit down,' hissed Charity, rattling down the corridor with a dustpan and brush.

'You sit down and you not touch anything.' She swept briskly in case Memsahib should get up.

'You just sit, you hear me?'

Though her sight was poor, Charity's sister had a keen sense of smell which soon located the pile of dirty nappies. She rinsed them in the sink, blocking the waste pipe. Charity came to the rescue once more, but even she could hardly keep up with the mounting chaos.

Her sister's efforts with the baby met with more success. Her habitual clumsiness gave her an innate understanding of anything weak or helpless. But Memsahib demanded more than that, she demanded perfection.

Memsahib frowned at the washing line, at the blemishes large and small that Charity's sister could not even see. The coup de grâce came as a relief to Charity. She yearned for the peace of two days ago.

Once more the best of friends, Simeon unlocked the store cupboard and giggled with Charity as they made a premature start on next week's rations.

Ayah finished packing. There was not much to do since Memsahib owned the furniture, though someone less scrupulous would have taken everything. Memsahib had been kind enough to give Ayah one or two dresses she no longer wore and Ayah also had a large collection of tins and bottles she had salvaged from the dustbin. They would be a present for her mother.

Ayah had one plate and one cup which she had brought from an Asian shopkeeper. They had given her much joy though the gilt edging was fast fading. There were pink roses around the brim, just like the ones in Memsahib's garden.

On the walls, Ayah had some pictures torn from old magazines. Her favourite was of a white woman holding a naked baby which was strange since all white people were rich. She couldn't see whether the baby was a boy or a girl because of the length of white drapery but Ayah decided it was a girl, like Susan with soft curly hair. The mother was beautiful too, in a lovely blue dress with grey eyes and long dark hair which hung loose on her shoulders. It reminded Ayah of Memsahib. Ayah decided to take just that one picture.

Even so few belongings presented a problem with the baby. She could tie her possessions in her kitengi and carry them on her head. But she needed the cloth to tie her baby to her. If she used the towel for the luggage and tied her baby naked on her back, then she had nothing with which to protect him from the midday sun.

'I give you bag,' said Simeon, but the price was too high.

Ayah took her son and her problem to Memsahib. Memsahib looked black. She had changed her baby, fed her baby, sung to her baby, not a dreary two-toned lullaby but Brahms's cradle song in German, in a rich contralto. Still the baby cried. Memsahib's voice cracked and she wept.

Ayah crept up the verandah steps, put her baby on the table and laid the white garments next to him. She held out her arms towards Susan and lifted her from her mother's shoulder. Susan inhaled the aura of her ayah and went limp to the sound of the soft dark voice.

'Sleep, sleep, Susan sleep.'

Susan and Ayah went into the nursery. The boy cried on the table top, a newborn cry like the call of a kite. Ursula stirred at the sound and picked up the child. He nuzzled at her breast and she yearned to comfort him.

The towel slipped and Ursula saw with horror that the child was naked. She slid the white vest back over his curly head, pinned on a nappy and straightened the gown.

Susan's ayah peering through the door was puzzled. She walked timidly onto the verandah. Ursula looked at Ayah over the small black head. The two women smiled, acknowledging their need of each other.

CHAPTER 5

'I will call him Isaac,' said Ursula. The name came to her during a dream. Afterwards the dream escaped her but the name was on her lips when she woke. Isaac, meaning joy and laughter, a son born when hope was gone. He was very special to her from the moment of his birth. She was the first person to touch him and she feared that his mother would not care for him as well as she would herself.

Ursula had brought him into the world and it seemed to her that this had created between them a bond stronger than that of physical kinship. He was her child in a way Susan could never be. Instinct had prompted her to reach out for Isaac, when he was born, even though she had never touched a black person before. Once she had touched him she realised there was nothing to be afraid of. She was not like her mother, spending her whole life in a provincial English seaside town with the firm assumption in her head that all blacks were dirty. Ursula had for three years been surrounded by black servants, cooks, chauffeurs, cleaners, ayahs, gardeners. Even the policemen were black. After a short time in the country, Ursula discovered to her amazement that not only had she ceased to notice that all menials were a different colour from herself. She no longer noticed them at all. She felt infinitely superior to her mother.

So life returned to normal. Susan was happy, so were her parents. Ursula saw that life was just as it always had been.

From Ayah's point of view things would never be quite the same again. Now Isaac came to work with his mother and shared Susan's pram and Susan's clothes. They lay at opposite ends of the pram, one dark, one light, smiling up at the black and white faces that loomed into view.

Ursula sat on the verandah and basked in the warmth of her family. George was happy that his wife was happy and was amused to see the two babies together.

There was now one and a half times more work for Ayah. The load was not quite doubled for though Isaac was a white baby by day, at night he slept naked, wrapped in a pile of rags on the floor.

Once more in the afternoons Ayah strolled with the pram under the trees by the stream. Shamba waited for her there. For days she ignored him, then she teased him, still hurt by the way he had treated her. But the day came that while the babies slept he took her among the bullrushes. He moved back into Ayah's room and kept his for his own private use. Afterwards he no longer needed to lie in wait, not for Ayah.

Ayah was glad that Shamba ignored her during the day, for she had a guilty secret. Deep down in the garden where the sun filtered warm through the canopy of leaves, she would set aside her crochet work and lean against a tree trunk with a child at each breast. It was easier than a long walk through the heat to the house when her babies were hungry.

The first time that she had fed Susan, Ayah was consumed by guilt. She feared she might have infected Susan with her own blackness. She had crept into the house, into Susan's room and there sat peering at the child until the sun rose on a Susan who was as pink and cream and golden as ever. Ayah told herself that in her small way she was repaying Memsahib for the food that she and Isaac received from Memsahib's table.

'Half past three, Memsahib,' said Ayah.

Ursula sighed and put down her sewing. The afternoons simply flew by, but she received her daughter graciously on her knee.

Susan cried when Ayah left. She had been happy in the

dappled shade with the grass soft under her rug. She had managed to roll over onto her front and struggled to within a hair's breadth of pulling enough material aside to scrabble her fingers among the green blades.

Ursula did not like babies who cried. She spread Susan's mat on the floor and arranged her toys round the edge, plastic animals that squeaked and brightly coloured rattles to shake or chew.

Charity brought a tray of tea and placed Susan for Memsahib in the centre of the blanket. Susan held her head high and looked to the lawn beyond the verandah. She elbowed aside the gaudy toys and felt the cold concrete hard against her stomach.

Ursula picked up her tea and waited for Susan to settle down. She sewed, trying to ignore the noise, then passed through varying stages of irritation which exploded at last into anger. Picking up her flaxen-haired angel, Ursula marched down the garden and dumped her on the lawn with Ayah and Isaac.

Susan felt her mother's anger and her body stiffened in fright. Her mother's love was suddenly infinitely more precious than her piece of grass. She wailed as she felt the prickly vegetation on her bare legs. She held up her arms towards her mother and wept for the warmth and safety she had lost.

Ursula marched indoors to write a letter, out of earshot of her daughter's crying. Her hands shook and she could not think what to say.

Ayah cuddled Susan. She sang and rocked backwards and forwards until Susan forgot her grief and reached out for the nearest leaf.

Ursula gave up the letter and stormed into the kitchen, just to keep the staff on their toes. The servants disturbed her constantly. Either she heard chatter which indicated frivolity when they should be going seriously about their duties, or there were the silences which she interpreted as tea breaks. Such intervals she pictured as punctuated by the chinks of tea cups as they sat on the doorstep drinking tea – *her* tea – liberally sweetened with *her* sugar.

The raid was entirely successful. Simeon paused, cup half-way to mouth. Charity sprang to her feet, giggling. Shamba held his cup behind his back. It was so childish.

Spleen vented, Ursula sailed back to the verandah to resume her needlework. Isaac now slept in a corner in a wickerwork basket. He slept fitfully these days, just for half an hour, at odd intervals. He was growing his first teeth and at times the pressure of taut skin over his gums was unbearable. He had learnt that it helped to press hard where it hurt, and he had achieved sufficient coordination to stuff everything he could into his mouth and bite hard.

Ursula saw the dark arms waving over the side of the crib. As Isaac started to cry she laid aside her work and draped him over her shoulder. Up and down, up and down, she walked in the shade, patting and crooning until Isaac was quiet. When Ursula sat down he cried, not because of the pain, as she imagined, but because he missed the gentle rhythm of her movement.

'Look George,' said Ursula proudly. 'Teeth!' Two tiny pearls jutted from Isaac's lower jaw.

'I have never seen such white teeth before,' said Ursula. George grunted into his newspaper.

Ayah was indoors changing Susan's dress. Susan was nearly one. She dribbled constantly, wetting her clothes under the chin. Ayah feared she might become sore and besides, she was anxious that Susan should always look her best.

Susan clung to the end of her cot, her legs planted firmly apart, sturdy legs with a dimple each side of each knee. She swayed backwards and forwards and smiled up at Ayah while her hair was brushed. She was so beautiful with her golden skin and fair wavy hair that Ayah took her into her arms.

Simeon stood in the doorway and watched. He had added perhaps a dozen new dishes to his repertoire, including Charity, but Ayah still eluded him. It was a serious blow to his ego but he was a patient man.

Charity swept with a new broom, blue-handled with bristles of soft yellow nylon. She ran her fingers along the brush head and it reminded her of Bwana's fields of corn rippling in the wind.

Shamba had new sheepskins for his feet. One of his jobs was

to polish all the floors in the house each Friday. Memsahib measured and hemmed the dish-cloths with which he applied the polish. Charity moved the furniture to ensure every square inch of wood received due nourishment. She held the long heavy curtains off the floor to keep them clean.

Shamba skated (energetically when Memsahib was looking) through the bedrooms, corridors, hall, study, living room and dining room. When the wood shone to a degree that was positively dangerous, Memsahib came to inspect. She looked under the beds, moved each chair and rug, fingered the hem of every curtain. Then she opened wide the windows to remove the smell of sweat.

Through the nursery window she watched Isaac in the garden. He stretched up his arms to catch the blossom drifting like purple snowflakes from the jacarandas. Isaac became more and more excited, his arms flailed wildly until he lost his balance and fell over backwards. He shrieked as his head grazed the rough bark of a tree trunk. It would have been so easy, thought Ursula, to foresee such an accident and put Isaac a foot further away, but that was the sort of thing she had to live with. Her friends did not seem to realise that back home, scrubbing their suburban villas.

Shamba spun into the wash-house on his sheepskin feet, stopping with a final twist and flourish in front of the large china sink. The wash-house was cool and white, the soapy water pleasantly warm. Shamba plunged the sheepskins under and squeezed until bubbles of air burst on the surface. He pummelled and squeezed until the surface of water was whipped to a froth.

He lifted one hand dripping with bubbles and held it up to the sun. Each bubble became a rainbow image of grass, trees, window and himself. Shamba laughed out loud and plunged his hands back into the water. Suds flew and reflected sunlight sparkled on the walls and ceiling. Shamba forgot his aching back.

Memsahib remained on the cool verandah until the house was thoroughly aired. She worried about Shamba – the way he smelt, his inefficiency, his lack of pride in his work. She studied the path he had worn across the lawn. However often she told him, he still followed the same track to the stream for water. He only needed to walk a little further with the heavy buckets to spare the grass.

Ayah and Susan played ring o'roses on the lawn. Atishoo, atishoo all fall down into the purple carpet of flowers. Isaac picked up a handful of petals and stuffed it into his mouth. Ayah stopped singing and bent down. She put her little finger into Isaac's mouth to hook out the mushy purple mess. Ursula hoped Ayah's hands were nice and clean, it was impossible to tell.

Indoors, Charity dusted the living room with a new duster as yellow and soft as a day old chick. She rubbed it along her cheek, then along the shelf. She frowned to see dust blacken the new cloth. Memsahib had so many things, baskets of shells, polished stones, glass animals, china figures in strange clothes unlike anything that Memsahib ever wore.

Ursula watched the clean dusters and skins swaying gently on the washing line and felt that all was as it should be. 'But why,' she wondered, 'are they content to live in such squalor at home. Why do they not learn from my example?'

Underneath, all was not as tranquil as the idle duster suggested. Ursula was not entirely happy. Her days were filled with cares, that was the lot of a white woman in the tropics she felt. There was always so much that needed doing but nothing that needed doing today.

Ayah too was troubled. She suffered at night when she had to revert to life as a black woman. She would have liked to be with baby Susan all the time, not just during the day. Her life was not easy in the servants' quarters. Simeon was a threat. She had never quite forgiven Shamba. Charity was jealous of the way Memsahib seemed to favour Ayah and give her things. If Ayah shared out her favours with the other servants then Memsahib was angry.

Ayah had nothing to replace the pleasures of chatting around a fire at night or of going to gather fruit or berries in the forest. She was happy to see Isaac dressed as a white boy but in the evenings could not let him crawl around in the dirt for fear he spoiled his nice clothes. She could not let him play with other children or eat posho out of a saucepan on the floor. Memsahib said he might catch something.

Isaac's father felt himself usurped as head of the family by a white woman. Of course, there were some advantages for his son. He also had problems in the shamba. Memsahib insisted on three vegetables for dinner but the garden adjoined the forest and the forest contained many deer. He built a wooden fence but the deer jumped over it. He set traps but Memsahib said that was cruel. He suggested hiring a toto, but Memsahib did not believe in child labour. Besides, the child would need to be paid. Wire netting too was expensive and Memsahib disliked expense. What could he do? Shamba squatted, resting his head on the handle of his panga while he thought what to do.

Ursula saw him from the bathroom window. Shamba was too preoccupied to notice the twitch of the net curtains. She thought it not surprising they were always short of vegetables when all Shamba ever did was sit around. She sat on the edge of the bath and re-read her letter.

'Why not bring Susan for a few days of civilisation? She could play with Naomi and we could shop and catch up on news.'

Ursula was tempted but there were obstacles. Could she manage Susan without Ayah? She could not take Ayah without Isaac. She could not take Isaac, not to Stephanie's. As she thought, the days became weeks and she was still undecided. It was so much easier to stay at home. But she wanted to go.

She turned to sorting out her wardrobe, to see if there was any justification for shopping. She had many dresses which exhaled mothballs and memories but few that were suitable for her present life. When had she last worn a long evening dress? In the tropics Ursula wore only cotton, long for evening, short during the day. Artificial fibres were unbearable in the heat but the unsuitable clothes were too good to throw away. She gave them to the servants. If ever she returned to England, she thought, they would in any case be out of fashion.

That night Ayah slept in an emerald green, long-sleeved, tricel dress with a tight frill round her neck. It was uncomfortable but at five and a half thousand feet the nights were cold and she had only one blanket. The dress became crushed during the night when Shamba dragged it up around her waist. Ayah lay very still, worrying that it might be spoilt. It was a tribute to synthetic textiles that by the time she had pattered barefoot to the toilet, washed last night's dirty pans, lit charcoal and brewed the tea, all the creases had hung out. Apart from the sweat stains under the arms and her square bare feet, Ayah looked ready for any garden party, even though she persisted in wearing a cotton handkerchief around her head when a real hat would have been much more suitable. But Ursula had given Charity the hat which matched the green tricel. Charity wore it while she swept out her bedroom with a short twig-broom, wearing a pale pink nightdress.

Then, quite suddenly, Ursula decided she would go away, and set a date. The whole household was turned upside down by the forthcoming departure, such an event had not occurred before.

George wanted to stay at home, though he offered to drive Ursula and Susan into Nairobi and return the same day. To whom could he entrust his fattening, cross-bred beef stock? On whom could he rely for more than one day? Yet he had good herdsmen who had spent their lives on the plains. But their herds were made up of tough, scrawny animals who could scratch a living from the desert floor and had little value to the white market which demanded its steak rare and tender.

Simeon would stay behind to look after Bwana. Taking no risks, Ursula drew up a list of meals in duplicate, one copy for the cook and one for her husband. She told Simeon to empty and scrub the larder and to study his recipe books in any spare time.

Charity was to wash blankets, air mattresses and carpets, polish the brass, wash curtains and ornaments and re-line Memsahib and Bwana's bedroom cupboards with clean newspaper.

Shamba would whitewash the verandah and paint the garden furniture. When that was done, he was to clear a hundred-yard strip of forest to extend the vegetable garden.

Ayah was told to take a holiday.

'I not want holiday, Memsahib,' she wailed. 'I want come with you and look after Susan.'

'You must look after your son,' said Ursula and hoped Ayah would do so well. She could find nothing else for her to do. It would be Ayah's first holiday in the two years that she had worked for Memsahib. She had had the occasional half day when George was not working, but Ursula could not contemplate a whole day without Ayah.

Ayah viewed her approaching holiday with desolation and dreaded each day as it dawned.

CHAPTER 6

At last Memsahib was gone. It was an emotional moment. Isaac cried and Susan cried, her face a small, pale blob in the back window as the car accelerated down the drive. Ayah put on a smile for the sake of the occasion until the car was swallowed up in a cloud of dust.

Simeon laughed and threw his hat into the air. He chased Charity round the flowerbed. Shamba stood looking after the car as dejected as Ayah. He thought of all the work he had to do and how hard it would be for him to cheat.

'Tea time,' said Simeon. He made a pot of tea and took fresh rolls from the oven for the workers. Ayah was on holiday so she wasn't offered any.

Charity, Simeon and Shamba kicked off their shoes and relaxed on the back doorstep. They could have chosen anywhere in the garden, down by the lake, under the jacarandas or even the verandah. The ugly concrete yard sandwiched between the dustbins and the woodpile felt homely.

♦

George drove along the road which led in an easterly direction across the floor of the Rift Valley. Beyond the herds of impala and Thompson's gazelle loomed Mount Kenya, its twin snow-capped peaks appearing and disappearing through a halo of cloud. Ursula decided it was time to stop for coffee.

'What about here?' said George jamming on the brakes. 'There's a lovely view.'

'No shade,' replied Ursula.

While the other servants lounged in the sun, Ayah decided to take her son to meet his grandmother. Simeon and Charity watched in amazement as she emerged from her room in a long evening gown of primrose-yellow silk and high-heeled shoes. She had to fold down the backs to get her feet in, for her feet were wide and strong. Barefoot, Ayah could walk for days, now she stumbled and tottered towards Susan's pram. She tied Isaac in, under the sunshade. He waved to his father as he was wheeled away.

Shamba was proud of this entourage. He knew that no one else, not even Simeon, had such a splendid wife. Mother and child made good progress on the drive. By leaning on the pram handle, Ayah could ease the pressure on her feet.

Simeon and Charity began to giggle, then laughed out loud when one of Ayah's shoes fell off. Isaac's mother held her head high and did not look back.

'Here's a better place,' said George pointing to a pool of shade beneath the umbrella of a large acacia. A family of giraffe looked down on the car as it slowed down. Mount Kenya disappeared behind a scrubby hillock strewn with boulders and candelabra trees.

'No view,' replied Ursula. Like her mother, she enjoyed a picnic with a view. George accelerated and drove on.

♦

Isaac's mother arrived where the path to her village branched away from the driveway. The path was wide enough for bare feet in single file, even for an occasional bicycle, but two wheels abreast had never trundled that way before. The wheels lurched over tree roots, twigs caught in the spokes. Isaac screamed as the pram jolted from side to side, tossing him about like a cork in high seas.

'Here's just the spot,' said George as the car climbed the steep eastern wall of the Escarpment and the Rift Valley opened up beneath them.

'But there's no grass, where could we sit?' asked Ursula peering through her headache and dark glasses, her lips tightly compressed.

'You could sit on a stone.'

'But what about snakes. You never know what may be underneath a stone.'

'We'll never find anywhere at this rate.' George sighed and started the engine.

Ursula thought longingly of lush green grass on which the rug would float, then settle in a soft cushion as you sat down. Grass was necessary for the ideal picnic, as well as a view, and shade.

Isaac was slapped by his mother because she was hot and cross and he would not stop screaming. Isaac went very quiet. He had never been slapped before. He held his breath and clutched his arm in disbelief.

'Stop here, George,' said Ursula. The car tyres screeched and George backed up to the place his wife had indicated. It was an idyllic spot with grass and shade and below the vast lunar landscape of the Rift Valley, pock-marked with extinct volcanoes and jagged hills like slumbering dinosaurs. He turned off the engine and put one foot out of the car. Immediately they were surrounded.

'You buy sheepskin?'

'You want basket?'

'This very good rhubarb, Bwana.'

Susan shrieked as the car rocked and a sea of faces blacked out the sunlight. Through the open window a stream of tourist crafts poured onto Ursula's lap.

'Drive on,' she shouted.

George drove on while Ursula flung the unsolicited goods out of the window. Vendors ran after the car still hoping for a sale and scooping up their valuables from the tarmac.

'Too many people,' said George.

Isaac was hot and thirsty, so was his mother. She had not thought to bring a picnic. Today, after two hours travelling, they were not even half-way along a journey that usually took an hour and a half.

Ayah pushed the pram among the trees, out of sight, and picked up Isaac. He was eighteen months old and not yet weaned. She slipped the low-cut dress off her shoulders and held the toddler to her breast.

When she readjusted the dress it was torn from cleavage to navel. She blamed Isaac but fortunately her petticoat was held up by a pin. The pin dislodged the velvet violets which Isaac picked up and fingered, then chewed to a small pulpy mass. Ayah tied Isaac on her back with the pram sheets and he liked the novel mode of transport.

It was Susan who ultimately decided where her parents should stop. She was out of nappies and needed to go to the toilet. George slammed on the brakes and Ursula looked in dismay at a rocky ravine devoid of vegetation.

Susan screamed because her mother slapped her. Her knickers were wet because she should have taken them right off to pee but Ayah always helped her and Ayah was not there.

George spread a rug on the flinty ground. Ursula draped Susan's pants over the aerial to dry, put on her hat and poured coffee. It was too hot to eat but George said they really could not stop again or they would never get there.

♦

Two hours after she left home, Isaac's mother ripped off her shoes and flung them into the bushes. She looked at the puffy grey skin on one foot, and the blood on the other, and thought that perhaps it was not so easy to be a white woman after all.

Ursula rummaged through the small bag Ayah had packed for the journey. There were no dry pants because Susan never needed dry pants when she was at home. George began to unpack the boot for Susan's suitcase.

'Does she really need it?' he asked.

'She can't arrive with a bare bottom,' snapped Ursula. Susan's socks were wet too. Susan whinged and whined and spilt her orange juice.

'Be quiet,' wailed Ursula, 'or I'll give you something to cry about.'

Ayah wiped her face with the pale silk hem of her dress. The shiny material scratched her skin and smeared the sweat without absorbing it. But the village was in sight.

Ursula took a cool, wet flannel from her sponge bag. She mopped her forehead, dabbed on some powder and combed her hair. It clung and straggled down the back of her neck, so she coiled the heavy mass and pinned it on top of her head. She re-packed the suitcase and the uneaten picnic and George re-packed the boot.

Susan slept, flushed and crumpled on the back seat for the rest of the journey.

When Susan's Ayah arrived at her home children rushed out to touch her dress. Men shook their heads and marvelled. Her son, in shorts, T-shirt, shoes and socks was admired like a little doll. They wanted to play with him, but he clung to his mother's skirt and would not let go.

Ayah wished she had kept her shoes as she progressed

through the village like the Pied Piper. She reached her mother's hut but only found her brothers and sisters. She had not been home for two years and they did not remember her.

Ayah should have remembered that only the young and the old would be in the village at that time of day. She made her way towards the mealie plantation. The children scampered ahead and as Ayah reached the edge of the shamba a figure straightened up from the row of bent women. Ayah realised that the near naked person was her mother and felt ashamed for her.

The old lady greeted this daughter who had risen from rags to riches and patted her grandson on the head. She had never seen such a plump and healthy child before. He was too heavy to carry all day long on her back though. She laughed and shook her head and tried to speak to Isaac but he did not understand her language.

The two women sat in the shade and stared at one another, lost for words. They looked at the dusty view and shared a sip of tepid water from a vegetable gourd. Ayah did not let Isaac drink. The water was unboiled, from the river.

A girl staggered up with a wailing bundle tied to her back. Isaac's grandmother unwrapped it and put it to her breast. It was a thin sickly baby.

Ayah pulled down her dress to feed her child who was not hungry. Isaac plucked and pinched at his mother's plump breast and tweaked her nipple between his teeth. She flinched and pulled up her dress.

Ayah's mother laughed and suggested she might feed her baby brother instead of her son. Ayah looked at the baby's match-stick arms and legs. It smelt of the cattle and goats that shared the family hut. She shook her head, and said 'No'.

George stopped the car and hooted in front of a high white gate topped with barbed wire. A uniformed guard saluted and jangled a large bunch of keys. Gravel crunched under the tyres and the front door opened at precisely the moment when the car stopped.

Memsahib Stephanie arose from her chair in the shade of the

verandah. Her heels clattered on the tiled floor. She patted her dress and shook her hips so that her skirt hung smooth over her petticoat.

'Ursula darling, you must be exhausted.' The two women pecked one another on the cheek.

'And George, how are you?' George reeled in the aura of powder and perfume and gripped Susan's hand tightly.

'This is Susan,' he said, but she hid herself behind him and peeped through his legs.

'I'll ring for some tea. You must be quite dehydrated.' Stephanie rang the small silver bell which stood on a small glass-topped table flanked by African violets and sea shells. Ursula looked around the verandah with envy. It was large enough to warrant being called a room, open to the garden on one side, deep and cool and exotic.

'Where are the children?' asked George. Stephanie shrugged and the tea appeared silently with a slice of lemon on each bone-china saucer.

Isaac's mother decided they would go home rather than stay for the night. She was sorry to see the hurt in her mother's eyes but she felt weak and had a headache. Ayah was not used to being out in the sun all day and had missed her mid-morning coffee and biscuits, lunch with the children and afternoon tea on the lawn. She scuffed her toes and looked down at the patterns in the dust as she said goodbye.

'Why don't you go with Ayah?' said Stephanie to Susan. 'You could play with my children.' Susan clung to her father's legs and buried her face in his lap.

'She's all right with me,' said George and lifted her onto his knee.

'I thought you might like your tea in peace,' laughed Stephanie, 'after the long drive.'

'She's no trouble.'

'Tea?'

'Yes please. With milk.'

Stephanie rang the bell. Ursula wiped lemon juice off her fingers and looked at the thick green turf over which sprinklers sent a continuous fine spray.

George and Susan drank their tea and wandered down the garden. They ran underneath the sprinklers, laughing at the feel of the water cold on their bare legs.

Ursula wished George would go.

George hadn't changed a bit, thought Stephanie. She had always rather fancied George. He had such a sense of life and fun, whereas Ursula . . .

The two women sat in silence.

'You've changed your hair,' said Ursula suddenly, desperate for something to say.

'Well, you haven't seen me for two years.'

'I meant the colour.'

'Stephen says it takes years off me.'

'It's not just bleached by the sun then?'

Stephanie laughed and shook her arms above her head so that her bracelets jangled.

'You were like this when I last saw you,' Stephanie indicated with her arms a grotesque bulge of stomach. 'Like an elephant,' she chuckled.

Ursula was pleased to catch sight of a slight fuzz of hair in Stephanie's armpits. Stephanie abruptly lowered her arms. They watched George with Stephanie's three children under a tree. He handed the elder boy a cricket bat and began the run up to bowl. George was still very athletic, thought Stephanie, compared with Stephen. She eyed Ursula's stomach thinking that two years was the average between the first two children.

'When will you have another?'

'Another what?' asked Ursula.

'Baby.'

Ursula shrugged and helped herself to more tea. She wondered whether to tell Stephanie about Isaac and decided against it.

'George is in his element with a lot of children,' remarked Stephanie.

♦

'Won't you stay for dinner?' Stephanie asked George who sprawled in a chair with a glass of beer. She had sudden misgivings about two weeks of undiluted Ursula.

'I must get back,' replied George. He drained his beer and sprang to his feet thinking of his workmen and his cattle. He was flattered though by the regret in Stephanie's face. She was always so cheerful and understanding. He took her hand, said how sorry he was he couldn't stay, and was gone.

Ursula felt relieved of all responsibility. Susan was playing with the other children. There were no meals to plan or servants to chivvy. She could just relax and enjoy herself.

Shamba felt total despair as he looked at the site for the extended vegetable garden. His head ached after a whole day in the sun and the area of soil cleared was pitiful. Besides, the clearing of new ground was women's work, like planting and harvesting.

Simeon had not moved from the doorstep all day except to make more tea or relieve his bladder. His recipe book lay unopened. A man needed time for thought.

'You go clean larder,' he ordered Charity. It was not a man's job to clean and scrub.

While Simeon sat outside, Charity got her own back. She folded sheets of newspaper to make bags and filled them with rice, sugar, tea and lentils. She hid them in the copious pockets of her dress, underneath her apron.

George looked at his watch as he drove down into the Rift Valley. He would be home in two hours. He tried to remember what was on the menu for tea, was it curry, or beef olives?

Simeon stirred. It was time to cook Bwana's tea. He had already torn up the list of menus that Bwana had carelessly left on top of his desk. He would substitute meals of his own devising. Tonight there would be roast beef, for Simeon was having guests and the leftovers would serve admirably.

He weighed the joint. Five pounds. He feared he had not left himself enough time.

Ayah's mother was left shaking her head over the stranger who was her daughter, not knowing whether to be pleased or not.

Ayah hurried along through the dusk. Among the trees she felt nervous. Animals stirred in the undergrowth. Overhead there might be leopards.

It was quite dark by when she reached the place where she had left the pram. She wandered from the path, luminous in her primrose silk. Twigs scraped her arms and scratched her face but she had to keep looking. Somewhere there was Susan's pram.

Isaac could feel his mother's panic, her quick breathing and fast heartbeat. He wailed with fear. He wanted his meat and veg. His mother was winded by a hard spike that jabbed into her stomach. She nearly wept with relief when she realised it was the pram handle.

A huge orange moon rose, more threatening than total darkness. Shadows deepened. The chrome on the pram gleamed and so did the eyes of animals. A branch cracked and Isaac's mother spun round.

She dragged the pram back to the path and almost threw Isaac into it. His little fingers clung to the edge as they sped along but at a particularly violent jolt he lost his grip. Isaac toppled out and the pram overturned on top of him.

The smell of roast beef permeated the house. Simeon basted the joint regularly and turned the tin to ensure even browning. A whole tin of roast potatoes sizzled.

Charity laid the table for one and added a small bunch of garden flowers. She went into the bedroom and tried on one of Memsahib's nightdresses. It was so beautiful. She had dreamt of this moment. The white lace at collar and cuffs showed to great advantage on Charity's skin. She dabbed talcum powder on her face and was disappointed that the result was grey rather than white.

At dusk Shamba watered the roses and fed the hens. His day had been long and tiring and he returned to his room to find his wife was not yet back. He set about cooking his own supper which he had not done since Ayah had come to work for Memsahib. He added too much water to the maize meal. He added more meal and the porridge went thick and lumpy. He went to the tap for more water while the posho burnt to a thick black mass on the bottom of the pan.

George was surprised to see Ayah careering wildly along the drive with her yellow silk dress tucked into her pants. Isaac could just be seen, clinging to the sides of the pram, bawling.

George hooted and swerved past, showering the pair with dust. If it had not been for the pram Ayah could have stepped off the road into the bushes until the dust died down. It drifted into Isaac's wide open mouth and he choked and spat. He rubbed his knuckles into his eyes, filling them with dust, and roared even louder.

Charity saw the headlights and just had time to remove Memsahib's nightdress, wash her face and rinse the powder down the sink in the time it took George to park the car. As he walked up the front steps Charity flung the door open and greeted him with a smile.

Simeon bustled up the corridor to bring Bwana an iced lager to drink in the shower. He had added ice cubes because Bwana would be hot and thirsty after the long journey. He had added so much ice that there was not room for all the beer. Simeon sipped the remainder as he carved the joint. George usually carved but it would save him the trouble and Simeon did not want him to see the size of the joint.

Simeon hovered over the serving dish adding a sprig of parsley here and there.

♦

'I thought it was curry tonight.'

'Oh no. Bwana make mistake.'

'Beef olives then?'

Simeon shook with laughter.

'Bwana, you look on the list of Memsahib.' But though George searched everywhere after dinner, the menus were nowhere to be found.

Isaac and his mother arrived home while George was drinking his coffee. Ayah was too weary to cook. She scraped some posho off the bottom of the pan but Isaac would not eat it. He spat it out, yelling for his beef and gravy and roast potatoes. Ayah smelled the roast meat and watched Simeon serve his friends, but no one offered her any. She closed the door and tried to sleep. Isaac slept fitfully, demanding from his mother more and more of the milk that was no longer enough for his growing body.

CHAPTER 7

'Let's go shopping,' suggested Stephanie over breakfast.

'Why not?' replied Ursula, for this was what she had come for.

Followed by the chauffeur carrying a wire basket they wandered through the supermarket.

'Isn't it wonderful that you can get soya sauce now? I'll put in a couple of bottles for you.'

'George doesn't like Chinese food.'

'That is exactly what Stephen said when I married him.'

Stephanie halted in front of a vast pyramid of breakfast cereals. She consulted her list.

'What would you and Susan like?'

'We just have cornflakes at home.'

'How dull. I'm sure she'd like these. And these. My children love them.'

The chauffeur went back to collect another basket.

'Vegetables next,' announced Stephanie. Ursula wove after her friend like a sleepwalker, confused by the noise and the dust and the people.

'I love this shop,' confided Stephanie. She paused to peel a banana off the shelf and hand it to a grey parrot that squawked just behind them, making Ursula jump. Rows of vegetables stretched before them, a cornucopia of the fruits of every season.

'You do like asparagus, don't you?'

'It doesn't look fresh to me.' Ursula prodded a pale limp stalk.

'Oh. What about ratatouille for dinner then?'

'It would be all right for cooking.'

'It's the heat you know. We haven't all got our own shambas.'

In spite of Memsahib's absence day dawned on the farm. The household arose at the usual time and breakfast was served promptly at seven-thirty, a vast plateful of bacon and eggs.

'Is this all for me?' George inquired.

'Oh Bwana,' chuckled Simeon, waddling from the kitchen. 'Memsahib she cross with me if you not eat.' He leant on a chair back and waggled his finger.

'I'm tired,' said Stephanie. 'What about coffee at the club?'

'That would be nice.' Ursula stared at a tray of anaemic eggs and remembered something she had forgotten to tell Simeon.

Bwana had departed with his truckful of labourers. Simeon sat down in the dining room for his breakfast.

'Charity, you bring tea and sugari,' he shouted. In the middle of a mouthful the phone rang.

'Memsahib, she want speak you,' called Charity. Simeon hid

his white table napkin behind his back and went to the phone.

'Oh jambo, Memsahib.'

'Jambo. It's about the eggs, Simeon. Don't waste any fresh eggs. You must make cakes and put them in the freezer.'

'But Memsahib, you take key to freezer.'

'Well, ask Bwana to give you the key this evening. You can take out meat for tomorrow and put the cakes in.'

When Ursula returned to her friend a large silver coffee pot stood on the table. Stephanie lay on a sun bed in her bikini.

'Bleaching my hair,' she giggled. Ursula sipped her coffee and felt uncomfortably hot in the small circle of shade beneath a thatched macouti roof.

'Darling, why don't you change?' Stephanie rummaged in her bag and produced another bikini. 'Try this.'

Ursula looked at the bright stripes and the small quantity of material and declined.

Isaac's mother sidled into the kitchen.

'Please, I have bread?'

Simeon shook his head.

'Memsahib she not tell me.'

'Isaac not want posho,' said his mother, her arms hanging limply by her side, head bowed. Isaac had screamed for his weetabix and toast and lightly boiled egg.

'Why you not take from nursery?'

'Is locked.' The whole nursery wing was locked, the small kitchen, bathroom, bedrooms and washing room.

'She put key in pocket,' wailed Ayah.

'I help you,' said Simeon drawing himself up to his full height. He was a kind-hearted man who didn't like to see children suffer if it could be avoided. He rattled the door handles and peered through the locks. He inspected all the windows but Memsahib had been very thorough.

'You be kind to me, I help you,' he offered. He would be only too happy to help out. He could so easily be persuaded. Isaac's mother returned to her baby empty-handed. Principles were important, Memsahib said.

♦

Stephanie was joined by two friends in an equal state of undress.

'Ursula, make up a four for bridge,' called Stephanie.

'I don't play.' Ursula wished she had brought a book or some sewing. She sat with her hair tied back in a pony tail.

'Shall we go and look at some clothes?' But Ursula thought of the heat burning through the soles of her shoes, the traffic fumes and the synthetic fabrics Stephanie would have in mind.

'Not today. Have your game of bridge.'

'But we need a fourth.' The friends sat, watching the entrance to the pool. Stephanie would have enjoyed the challenge of brightening up her friend, with something cheerful and slightly frivolous. Then she would persuade her to lie in the sun so that she looked less like a marble statue.

Ursula sweated and worried. Had she really heard Isaac crying while she spoke to Simeon? She wondered what could have made him unhappy. Perhaps he was missing her? Perhaps he was crying for her.

Shamba was waiting for Ayah outside the kitchen door. He ordered her off to the vegetable garden to clear the ground for Memsahib's return. She had nothing else to do and it was women's work. Ayah tied Isaac on her back, and set off with her pangas. She was afraid to disobey Shamba.

Shamba whitewashed the verandah. It was a lovely job. Up and down went the wide bristles, slip slop and a splatter of fine spray that would not amuse Memsahib. Shamba stabbed carefully into every nook and cranny. Soon there was a large bright area that made the rest of the wall look grey. He sat back on the verandah railing, the better to survey his handiwork.

Simeon padded from the kitchen barefoot and hatless. He carried a tray of coffee and some little cakes hot from the oven. One of Bwana's cigarettes was propped on each ear. Shamba was overwhelmed at such generosity. He made himself comfortable in one of the chairs with his feet up on the railing. He ate and drank and smoked, just like Bwana, while Bwana was miles away in the scorching sun mending fences. He always took a sandwich and flask of coffee with him but felt uncomfortable eating in front of his men, who had nothing.

Charity hovered in the dining room with her duster, mindful of Simeon's instructions that Shamba must not leave the house.

Ayah was hot and tired. Isaac had grizzled all morning, asking for toast, for Memsahib, for Susan, for a drink. He asked for the moon and Ayah was at her wit's end. She carried Isaac to the side of the plot and plonked him down hard in the shade. She said she would beat him if he moved an inch or uttered a sound. After the day before, he believed her and sat quietly sucking his fingers.

Ayah worked efficiently. In half a day she cleared a larger area than Shamba managed in a day. She stood with her feet wide apart, body bent from the hips, and worked to a steady rhythm. If she had had company she would have sung while she worked. She had not sung since Susan left.

'A beautiful sight,' thought Simeon approaching unnoticed on his bare feet. He wore a clean hat and apron and carried a tray set with care. Memsahib had locked up the best silver but he had made do with stainless steel, made in Sheffield and polished on the corner of a tea towel. A crystal glass sparkled in the sunshine.

On a plate were choice pieces of cold roast beef, sliced avocado, green pepper and cool crisp lettuce. For Isaac there was weetabix and an apple. Simeon set the tray on a rug on the ground. It was the way Memsahib always arranged a picnic. Then he beckoned to the woman to come and eat.

Ayah was suspicious but Isaac had no scruples at all. Ravenous after his period of starvation he drained his orange juice at one go and then attacked the weetabix. Simeon said nothing, just watched and smiled like a cat.

Isaac's mother crept closer. She perched on the far side of the rug with the child beween herself and Simeon. She was parched and drained the glass of wine as if it too were orange juice. She ate the beef and salad and started to giggle.

Isaac slept with a full stomach. His mother felt drowsy and lightheaded and stretched back on the rug in the sunshine. The serpent whispered in her ear.

Simeon moved closer. His hand was on her knee, large and soft like unbaked dough. Shamba's hands were rough and calloused, he smelt of sweat and tasted of salt. Simeon's skin was like a baby's, scented with all the good things from Memsahib's kitchen, pies and pastry and a touch of seasoning.

Simeon was old and grey-haired and lay on her like a stranded whale. Ayah was young and warm and full of sunshine and wine. It was pleasant to relax and feel loved. Simeon was large and soft, life with him would be so easy. He was kind, he whispered, he would not beat her. He was rich. He would cherish her. He had wanted her ever since he first saw her.

On the verandah, Shamba drained the coffee pot, gathered the cake crumbs into a pile and licked the plate. Too late he thought of his son and his son's mother. He felt guilty and stood up. Charity saw him and hurried onto the verandah. She regaled Shamba with tales of Simeon's romantic exploits while Shamba smoked and shook his head and laughed.

After lunch, Ayah carried the lunch tray down to the house in the footsteps of her Lord and Master. She went into the kitchen and washed up while Simeon carried rolls and butter onto the verandah for Charity and Shamba.

Ayah decided that her new relationship would be different from her liaison with Shamba. Simeon had his other wives, old Wambui who shared his room and young Mumbi back in his village while Ayah's position as 'wife' had neither legal nor tribal ratification, but she saw that for her sake and Susan's she must be in command of the situation.

Old Wambui was a problem. Her advanced years demanded that she take a pride of place which relegated Ayah to the status of junior wife.

'You must send Wambui away,' said Ayah.

Simeon bowed his head in agreement. What need had he of scrawny Wambui now that the lovely Ayah would take her place, to cook and clean and warm his bed? Let Wambui take the bus back to the village and till his shamba and help Mumbi with the children. Mumbi, though in no way Ayah's equal in beauty, caused Simeon much concern. She had cost many sheep and goats. Wambui could keep an eye on the girl in his absence. In the evenings, she could sit with the other old folk in the village and chat. He would really be doing her a favour. Yes, Wambui should leave at once.

Though Ayah had cost Simeon no more than the trouble of preparing a meal with Memsahib's ingredients, she insisted on being valued. Her wages were equal. She could read and write. She knew the ways of a white woman and Simeon wanted her.

Ayah demanded the keys to Simeon's room, moved her bed in and placed it next to her husband's. They would sleep in style, like Bwana and Memsahib. Isaac could sleep in the bed vacated by Wambui. Ayah heaped Shamba's belongings outside the door of his own room and fastened her door with one of Simeon's padlocks.

Then Ayah bolted Simeon's door on the inside and slept away the afternoon. She was awoken by Simeon bringing tea and buns. Ayah felt vaguely uneasy on awakening about what had happened but she reflected that Memsahib had never had her principles so sorely tested. Isaac was well fed and happy, and of that Memsahib would surely approve.

'Is that all?' George looked down at the small shreds of meat on his plate. Simeon thought of Ayah's strong white teeth chewing so delightfully in the sunshine.

'Well Bwana,' he remarked confidentially, 'that meat, she shrink in offen.'

Shamba chewed lumpy posho on his own and vowed revenge. So much had happened in one day that could have been avoided if Memsahib had not deserted her post.

CHAPTER 8

'You must let me take you home, I insist,' said Stephanie. She meant that she would ask Stephen whether they could have the car and chauffeur for the day. Ursula looked forward to returning to her own home, to a place where she was in complete control.

They were as usual having lunch at the club. Sitting alone at home with Ursula contained too many silences for Stephanie. Silence made her nervous. She always wondered what the other person was thinking.

'I think the company has done Susan good,' she remarked.

'She seems to be enjoying herself.' Ursula looked aghast at her naked daughter shrieking around the lawns.

'She was so quiet when she came,' laughed her friend, 'so timid. And then those big staring eyes . . . more like one of the servants' children.' Stephanie raised herself on one elbow and sipped her drink.

'She could do with more company at home as well.'

'She has Isaac.'

'And who is Isaac?'

Ursula wished the name had not slipped out.

'He can't be white, not with a name like that. It sounds like some ghastly missionary name. You should be careful you know. Don't encourage too much familiarity.'

Stephanie lay back and let the sun glimmer red through her eyelids. Ursula felt Isaac like a warm dark glow at the back of her conscience. She should have brought him with her and faced up to her friend. She should have acknowledged him just now and defended him, but she hid him like a guilty secret, like Peter in the Garden of Gethsemane.

'Oh, Isaac is just my ayah's child who plays with Susan sometimes. There are no white children within easy reach.' Even as she spoke Ursula heard the cock crow.

'Why don't we make the journey into a real adventure?'

'But it will be very hot and dusty.'

'We could go through the Game Park and stop off for lunch and a swim.'

'I really don't want to put you to so much trouble. George could easily come and fetch us.'

'Nonsense. It'll be fun.'

'No. I will ring George.'

'For once you are away from home. What's the rush to get back? You might not escape for another two years!'

So, they travelled via the Game Park. Ursula kept working out how much nearer home they would be if they had gone direct. Susan wanted to be home too. Her days had been hectic, full of activity and excitement which eventually dispelled the sick feeling with which she awoke in a wet bed with no daddy to run to, or ayah.

At home, Simeon and Charity enlisted Ayah's help with all the tasks that should have been done, but had been left until the last possible moment. They dragged Memsahib's best Persian rug onto the lawn and attacked it with hot soapy water and scrubbing brushes. Dismayed to see it look like a rather matted, mangy dog they summoned Shamba with the hosepipe to see if he could make it look any better.

Shamba had hired two village boys to clear the strip of garden. They giggled a lot and rested frequently in the shade, their legs protruded like those of storks' and their ebony potbellies gleamed with sweat. Shamba wondered whether his offer of two shillings a week had not been somewhat rash.

On the day of Ursula's return, George returned home unexpectedly for lunch anxious to be there to greet his wife and daughter. He came upon a scene of complete bedlam. The entire contents of the house seemed to be scattered over the lawn. Towering over the chaos was Simeon, magnificent in white, teetering on a pouffe while he waved his arms directing his troops.

'Take everything back indoors at once,' George roared, trying to imagine Ursula coming upon the scene.

'Bwana,' said Simeon with great dignity, 'when Memsahib come cross, I say we want work but you say no.'

At the Game Lodge, Ursula sat alone at a dining table. She watched a few listless elephants spout muddy water over their backs from an artificial pond. Nearly an hour ago Stephanie 'just popped in to see the hotel manager – such a very old friend' and had not yet returned. Ursula sipped her wine and picked at her dessert, a few tired slices of pawpaw and semi-liquid ice cream. She could have joined Susan at the pool but that would have been even hotter.

Susan dangled her feet in the water but was not allowed to swim, because Stephanie's ayah could not swim either.

'You take feet out,' shouted the attendant. He towered like a black giant above the sitting two-year-old, his head as tall as the acacias among a dizzying swirl of cloud. He indicated a notice which said that bathers could enter the water only after a shower and footbath to prevent dust from the road contaminating the water.

The attendant spoke for the benefit of the ayah to whom he wished to make his importance quite clear. Neither Susan nor the ayah could read, and nor could he. But Susan was frightened by the uniform and the enormity of her crime. She hid her face under the ayah's apron and wept.

All that morning Isaac slept, strapped into Susan's pram. He had diarrhoea from the sudden excess of rich foods since he had become Simeon's son. He would be happier and healthier when he returned to Memsahib's sensible, plain nursery fare.

Charity ironed curtains to dry them but there was no hope for the carpet. It would require at least two days of frequent turning in the sun before it could be placed on a wooden floor. Charity looked forward to Memsahib's return, perhaps imagining that life would return to normal. She still smarted from her demotion from being Simeon's woman.

Simeon was disposed to be especially kind to Charity. He even discussed with Ayah whether he should continue to sleep with her from time to time. He had his responsibilities as Head of the Household, and this he felt was one of them.

Shamba paid off his little labourers with deductions for idleness. They argued shrilly, but he impressed on them that as their employer he would tolerate no argument and he was bigger than they were. Shamba decided to finish the final yard of work himself after first resting in the sun. Then he could be hard at work when Memsahib arrived.

Stephanie returned to the table full of apologies and the hotel manager's sperm.

'There was so much to talk about Ursula, you can have no idea!'

Ursula had a very good idea as she noted the trembling hands and Stephanie's flushed cheeks.

'Waiter, the bill,' called Ursula and stood up. She would go and sit with Susan while Stephanie ate her lunch.

'There is nothing to pay, Memsahib.'

'Of course there is.'

'Oh no Memsahib. Bwana say you not pay.'

'I insist on paying.' Ursula gripped the edge of the table and her voice rose.

'Ursula, *please*,' said Stephanie.

'I must pay.'

The waiter scratched his head. Either he was in trouble with this memsahib, or he was in trouble with the manager. He wrote a bill on a torn off scrap of paper and brought it to Ursula on a plate.

'Keep the change,' said Ursula. She sat down again.

In a corner of the dining room the waiter slipped the money into his pocket. It was the equivalent of a month's wages. Unasked, he brought more coffee, smiling and bowing.

♦

Ayah scrubbed Isaac, shrieking, under the cold tap in the servants' yard. She could not use the hot shower because Bwana was at home. Then she tied Isaac back in the pram and set off to walk the three miles to the end of the drive. She wanted to be the first to greet Susan on her return.

The servants wore freshly laundered uniform to please Memsahib and impress her friend. George had a shower and flung his dusty farm clothes into the washing basket.

It was late afternoon by the time Stephanie's car reached the turning to the farm. Ursula saw Ayah sitting by the roadside with Isaac on her knee. Isaac waved and Ursula was happy. She wished she had the courage to ask Stephanie to stop the car, and again she heard the cock crow.

The car swirled into the drive spraying a red fan of dust behind it. Susan caught sight of Ayah and scrabbled over Stephanie's knee jabbing one elbow into a breast still glowing from the hotel manager's caresses. Stephanie slapped Susan hard on the leg without thinking what she was doing. Susan screamed and Ursula was outraged.

'Whore,' she hissed. There was a terrible silence in the car which persisted for the rest of the journey.

Ayah was showered with dust. Her apron ceased to be white and her dress was no longer crisp. Isaac stretched his hot, grubby arms in the direction of Memsahib's car. He had spent two hours crawling by the roadside and had soiled his dust-coloured pants.

Charity and Simeon wrestled in the front doorway, each anxious to be the first to welcome Memsahib home. Charity won, being more agile, and hurried down the steps, all smiles as she opened the car door.

George strode outside and gave each lady a peck on the cheek. It was more than Stephanie expected and less than his wife had hoped for. He sat on the doorstep with Susan limp and soggy in his arms, trying to find out the cause of her tears.

Ursula hurried to the toilet whence she could see the

vegetable garden. After a frantic bout of activity as the car sped up the drive, Shamba now squatted, resting his head on the panga handle. A familiar enough posture, thought Ursula, but was gratified by the amount of work he had completed. She dabbed cold water on her cheeks and returned to her guest.

The ladies took tea on the verandah served by a Simeon gloriously starched by his new woman. He was beginning to realise he had made an excellent exchange.

Ayah returned forty minutes later to a cold reception. Her place had been there at the house with the other servants, to greet Memsahib and assist with her child. Instead she arrived dusty and crumpled as if . . .

Ursula wondered whether Shamba was still idle in the vegetable garden or whether he could be held responsible for the crushed uniform. On the surface nothing had changed. Her home was just as she remembered it.

But below the surface much was different. It had nothing to do with the fact that Ayah was carrying Simeon's child, she did not know that yet. Ayah's wound went deeper. She had thought that she was Memsahib's friend, that Memsahib would welcome Isaac as her own son. She had set forth with love and devotion in her heart and had been ignored and covered with dust. Memsahib had turned her back on them both.

Ayah began to see that she was after all dispensible. It had happened before and it would happen again. Memsahib could not be relied on.

CHAPTER 9

'Daddy,' said Susan, 'please take me with you.' George who could refuse her nothing took her round the farm in his truck with his sweating labourers. Susan was nearly three. On the farm she wore shorts and T-shirts and suede safari boots and was baked brown and freckly by the sun.

'Like a boy,' thought her mother who insisted that at home Susan wore a dress and sun hat and sat in the shade.

Isaac would have liked to go in the truck too but he did not dare to ask Bwana. He stood and stared regretfully after the cloud of dust, then played on the verandah under the eye of Memsahib. Memsahib was happy to have him there while she sewed.

Isaac's mother washed and cleaned and ironed in peace while Susan was out. By the end of the day she felt her legs ache and her ankles swell and she worried about when this baby was born, and the next and the next.

George now took Susan out every morning and brought her home for lunch.

'It's not worth the trouble,' said Ursula thinking of the wasted petrol and time. Every lunchtime she had to remind herself how lucky she was to have had the morning alone with Isaac and that the sacrifice of lunch on her own was worth while.

After lunch George departed at ferocious speed while Ursula, Isaac and Susan retired to their shuttered rooms and slept. Ayah spent the afternoons on Memsahib's chair on the verandah, her aching feet perched on the verandah railing while she slept.

Ayah had become uncomfortably large this pregnancy. She

was beginning to move and look like Simeon. She no longer cleaned windows that were already spotless and only did what needed to be done. She realised that Memsahib didn't even notice. Simeon kept watch to bring Ayah a cup of tea and wake her as soon as he heard Memsahib stir.

Shamba watched her too as he polished his new lawn-mower. Now he was promoted to engineer he no longer minded the defection of his son's mother. He arranged the intricate maze of hoses and sprinklers designed to make Memsahib's lawn the envy of the area.

Shamba had persuaded Bwana to employ his two village boys to help him at his work. Shamba had instructed them to weed the flowerbeds. It was back breaking work. In the mid-day sun, their small fingers fumbled and ran with sweat and they pulled up everything that wasn't currently in flower. Shamba swore at them and wondered how he could have fathered such dolts. Everyone but Ursula, Susan and Isaac were aware of the relationship but no one mentioned it.

Charity came down the garden to peg out her dusters and Shamba deserted his post to enveigle her into the bushes. The boys giggled and took a rest while they looked admiringly at the clear patch of earth they had created.

On the back doorstep Simeon flipped through the pictures in his recipe book. Such recipes, lavish with brandy, cream and herbs! But what was this lobster that was no part of cow or sheep or hen or pig or fish as far as he could see? Simeon had heard tell in his childhood of the vast waters at the end of the land but he had never seen the sea.

In this way the household dreamed and slept away every afternoon until the end of the Kenyan summer.

Then the weather broke and so did Ayah's waters, considerately during the night. The baby was born swiftly, delivered into the hands of old Wambui who had been summoned back to attend the birth of her husband's child. Simeon was determined not to repeat Shamba's panic-stricken mistake and disturb Memsahib.

The baby was a girl, but so black thought Ayah. Her daughter's features betrayed her father's Kikuyu origins. She had none of the fine-boned, long-limbed look of her Masai mother.

Her nose was squashed flat like a boxer's, her arms and legs were short and stubby.

Simeon saw only beauty and happiness. He meditated upon her future as ayah for Memsahib's grandchildren, as a daughter to support him in his old age. He thought of bride prices guaranteed to keep pace with inflation. He considered his daughter as George might consider his investments, anxiously scanning the shares index of the *Financial Times*. She was a valuable property.

In his joy, Simeon cooked an extra large plateful of bacon and eggs for Bwana at breakfast. He understood now Bwana's tearfulness at the time of Susan's birth and knew that Bwana would likewise understand his own joy. Simeon was gratified by the response. Bwana put down his table napkin and shook Simeon warmly by the hand, looking straight into his eyes, man to man.

Five minutes later, when Ursula came to the table, George was absorbed in calculations. How many posts at intervals of a yard and a half were necessary to support five miles of barbed wire? He scribbled on a pad, frowned, crossed out and began again.

Ursula wondered why Ayah was late. She looked at her watch, frowned and decided that Susan had better have breakfast in the dining room. Ursula had had a battle getting Susan dressed. Susan liked to choose her own clothes every day, so did her mother.

'I want Ayah,' said Susan, flushed and swollen-eyed.

'She will be here soon,' replied her mother.

'I hate this skirt,' whined Susan. She could tell she was annoying her mother and knew she would soon be safely out in her father's Land Rover.

'These are horrid clothes. I hate them.'

Ursula had made them herself and it seemed a pity to waste good material like that.

'I won't be back for lunch today so Susan had better stay with you,' said George and hurried from the room.

Susan howled. Could no one be relied on? Such treachery from Daddy. Abandoned by Ayah. Her world crumbled around her. But mother remained. She picked up the squalling child, threw her into her bedroom and slammed the door.

Ayah arrived half an hour late, moving at a fraction of her usual speed. Her large square daughter had torn her badly, and the tear stretched and bled at each step. Without benefit of rest or stitches it would take a long time to heal.

Ayah had also been shocked into considering Simeon's appearance and origins in a way she had never done before. Previously she had seen him as a massive presence in an aura of whiteness or felt him as a vast blackness that was both reassuring and claustrophobic. In her child she saw his features clearly for the first time and was not altogether pleased.

At the nursery door stood Memsahib like a pillar of salt. She saw Ayah walking gingerly and decided that investment in malaria prophylaxis would pay handsome dividends during the rain. Ursula was not altogether unobservant. Ayah had been fattened during her pregnancy by delicacies smuggled from Memsahib's kitchen. Her baby had been large and in only six hours her distended stomach had not yet reverted to its normal size. She looked scarcely different from the Ayah of the night before.

'You are late.'

'Sorry, Memsahib. I want sleep too long.'

'You are not well?'

'Oh yes, Memsahib, very well.' Ayah remembered the drama following Isaac's birth. She waddled into the nursery to find Susan huddled in a resentful heap. Ayah put her arms around her milk-white child and wept.

Isaac, in the care of Wambui, looked at the sister who was responsible for his incarceration. As soon as the old lady left the room to make tea he slipped out of the door and headed for the verandah. No one would dare to touch him if Memsahib were there.

He took a roundabout route, avoiding Simeon at the kitchen window and ducked behind bushes when he saw Shamba. Shamba claimed familiarity with Isaac, but who was Shamba?

A person of no consequence to one who was now Son of Cook.

Simeon gazed from the window thinking with delight that his wife's body was his own once more. The body that was younger than some of his own children would warm him at night and ease him into his old age. Life seemed comfortable and good.

Deep down under the trees Ayah sat on the grass. Susan lay with her head on Ayah's knee and sucked her thumb. From far, far away came the soft chirrup of birdsong, from near came the click of Ayah's knitting needles. Susan's eyes closed and she slept.

Ayah was knitting a small white cardigan. Her baby would never need it but she felt better doing something for the child she knew she could never love. She thought of a young girl, daughter of a friend, who was now ripe for marriage. She would sew the seeds of desire in her husband's mind, it would not be hard to do with Simeon. Ayah would broach the matter with her friend in the certainty that Simeon would be an attractive proposition. Ayah would do everything she could to pass her sexual burden on to someone else. The cold shoulder and the sleeping back were weapons as unknown to her as other forms of contraception practised in western society.

Ayah knitted for her daughter and Ursula sewed for Susan. There were so many dresses that Susan would perhaps wear once, others that she would refuse to wear at all. For Susan liked the bright colours and patterns of locally printed cloth such as she saw Ayah wear in the evenings.

Ursula thought the attraction of a dress lay in its cut. It should provide a pleasant background for the wearer, like the setting for a jewel, rather than be an attraction in itself. Her own clothes were in such very good taste that they bordered on drabness, but then Ursula came from a culture in which clothes were taken for granted.

'Isaac,' said Ursula, looking up, 'I wondered what had happened to you today.' She smiled her first smile of the morning. She had been haunted of late by strange dreams in which she bore a child just like Isaac with olive skin and doe eyes who smiled with a flash of teeth. She laughed at the thought of a black child emerging from her womb.

'I have present for you, my memsahib,' said Isaac. Under the passion-flower vine on the septic-tank cover, hidden from all the world, Isaac had found a bright green grasshopper, about four inches long.

'Did you know, Isaac, that the ears of a grasshopper are in its stomach?' They both laughed.

Isaac put the grasshopper on the verandah railing and peered closely at its stomach. There were no ears, which disappointed him because Memsahib knew everything. She was always right. Perhaps she was teasing? He looked at her shyly.

The grasshopper sensed its exposure. It leapt towards the camouflage of green grass, trees and bushes. As it sailed through the air, it spread wings of a brilliant red like stained-glass windows with the sun shining through.

Isaac ran after his treasure which soon landed, for the grasshopper's wings are for balance and lift rather than flight. Before it had time to spring again, Isaac pounced. He carried it back to the verandah.

'What a good jump,' cried Ursula, clapping her hands and looking forward to a repeat performance. Isaac held the grasshopper in one hand and with the other snapped off its back legs.

'Now it will stay with us for ever,' he said. Shamba had shown him how to do that. He looked up proudly.

'Don't you ever do that again,' hissed Ursula. She felt sick.

Isaac looked at the grasshopper in his small hand. He had come through such perils bearing a gift, all for his memsahib. He put the insect down on the railing. It was unable to balance and toppled into the flowerbed below.

'I'm hungry,' said Isaac, who had had only posho for breakfast. He put his hand on Memsahib's arm and looked anxiously into her face. Ursula recoiled from the dark, cruel fingers and snatched her arm away.

'Memsahib, you come see my sister?'

'Your sister, Isaac?' Ursula looked at the figure now hanging out the washing. Slowly, so slowly it stooped and stretched, stooped and stretched.

♦

After lunch Memsahib suggested that Ayah took a rest on the verandah outside Susan's door while Susan slept. She would be in bed herself so it would cause no inconvenience to her.

As the days went by, Ayah felt permanently tired. Her baby daughter demanded food constantly, sucking her dry and still screaming for more. She refused all solids. Simeon was cross because the baby disturbed his nights and Ayah refused sex. She was still in pain since her tear had not healed and she was constipated from a fear of opening her bowels. At eighteen, Ayah could already foresee her body becoming like her mother's or sister's and dreaded becoming pregnant again.

Isaac, unaware of the problems that beset his mother, only knew that at times she was so short-tempered it was best to avoid her. Wambui was always available, squatting by the tap. He asked her to read to him, but she could not. He asked her to play, but she had never played. She expected him to sit and be quiet and not ask questions. She spat although Memsahib said that no one should spit, it was unhygienic. He told his step-mother this, she laughed and spat and called him 'Bwana Kidogo', little lord. She smelled.

So Isaac spent as little time in the servants' quarters as possible. Simeon took him back to his room each evening when dinner was served. If the dessert did not require last minute attention they left as soon as the main course was on the table.

Charity remained to clear the table and wash up and eat the leftovers if Simeon was not around. While Bwana and Memsahib ate she did her knitting. The wool was so bright it gleamed through the twilight. Charity was making a cardigan to wear over the skirt Memsahib had given her.

The evenings were Susan's favourite part of the day. With Isaac in the care of Wambui and her parents eating dinner, she had Ayah all to herself. Susan hid and Ayah looked for her.

'Susan, where is Susan? It is bedtime.'

Susan always hid in the clothes cupboard, right at the back behind the dresses, with the door open a crack so that it was not quite dark. Ayah looked everywhere. Could Susan be under the bed? Susan giggled. Was Susan behind the door? Susan shrieked 'No!' Could Susan be under the bedclothes? Susan stamped her feet and chortled with delight. Was Susan in the laundry basket? Ayah took off the lid, held her nose and shouted 'Poo'. Susan laughed and called out 'Course not, it's too smelly.' Was Susan, surely she would not be, in the cupboard?

Ayah groped her way along the pairs of shoes until she reached some with feet in them. Up the ankles and socks crept the fingers and Susan leapt out and threw herself on top of Ayah. They hugged one another till suddenly Susan went limp and put her thumb in her mouth. Ayah held her tight and sang her lullaby. Round and round the room they went and Susan reached up and twined her fingers in Ayah's tight black curls.

Then Ayah bent and laid Susan on her bed. She tucked in the covers and felt the milk streaming from her breasts. Her ugly daughter would be screaming with hunger.

The feel of the wet dress was unpleasant. Jagged brown circles on Ayah's white apron bib bore witness that this was not the first time today that Ayah had overflowed, not with love, for she looked in dismay at her child who drained her in enormous, painful gulps. Ayah feared wizened breasts, stretched by children who could be arranged in sizes as in one of Susan's little wooden puzzles. Only her children would never know what a puzzle was. Ayah felt a trap closing round her.

Simeon's girth increased. He moved more slowly, more pompously still. He had another daughter! He brought his child's mother titbits from the kitchen and stood over her while she ate. His child too would be strong and healthy.

Simeon removed the vase of plastic roses and the crotcheted cloth from the trunk that served as a table. He undid the three padlocks and rummaged through the contents until he came to the box that contained his savings. He was pleasantly surprised by the amount he found. It was more than he expected. He wondered how best to invest it, in cattle, sheep or a radio?

Ayah suggested another wife. In wives and children, she reminded him, lay his hope for a comfortable old age.

'Why I need new wife?' he asked and his hand crept up her leg. Ayah reminded him about his duties towards Charity. He was the head of the household and should be mindful of his position. Simeon knocked on Charity's door one night to be met by Shamba, and told rudely to go away. Simeon was taken aback by the incident, which he considered a slight to his dignity, but the germ of the idea of sharing out his sexual favours remained.

'But I want transistor radio too,' he wailed.

'You get wife, I buy you radio,' said Ayah. She smoothed her apron and felt in command of her life again. She went indoors and ironed Simeon's hat.

Memsahib insisted that everything should be ironed just as everything should be hung on the line to dry and not draped over the bushes or left on the grass. There was the danger of mango fly. The fly laid eggs under the skin of its host. The egg hatched into a maggot that wriggled and grew while the skin swelled and itched. The maggot pupated and emerged as a fly and the cycle was repeated.

Memsahib's family was safe. Her washing dried on the line and ironing was a further line of defence. But Ayah's daughter wriggled and squirmed and cried and her old stepmother continued to lay the washing on the grass.

CHAPTER 10

'Look Isaac, crocodiles!' said Susan. She held up the dark-hinged seed pod of the jacaranda between the fingers and thumbs of her two hands and ran after Isaac, making the crocodile snap its jaws. The case was the size of her palm, rough on the outside but inside smooth and golden, like satin to touch.

'Eat you up!' shrieked Susan.

'Snap, snap, snap!' squawked Isaac fleeing under the dusty canopy of trees.

Charity laughed as she watched in spite of the weather with all the windows open and not a breath of air. She swept and dusted the whole house every day only to find that half an hour after she had finished Memsahib would be complaining of dust again. There was also extra washing to be done since Memsahib insisted on clean clothes twice a day and on the servants changing their uniforms twice a week.

Ayah blinked at the washing line, almost blinded by the dazzle of white sheets and blankets from the nursery. She let the children play in the shade but never, never in the sun.

Ursula's life was not much affected at her post on the verandah.

'What are you doing, my memsahib?' asked Isaac, looking at the notebook and pencil.

'I'm planning Susan's birthday party.' Ursula ran her fingers through Isaac's curls, as sharp and springy as steel wool. Her little black lamb! Ursula had invited Stephanie to come and stay for a few days with her children and their ayah. Their quarrels on the day of the journey had been patched up long ago, since Ursula had no other friend she could stay with in town, and Ursula was Stephanie's only friend in the country. Besides, friendships formed during schooldays in another country were hard to break. Ursula imagined her house full of happy young faces.

In the kitchen, Simeon created wonderful soufflés and salads. It was too hot to eat anything more substantial. His strawberry ices had to be tasted to be believed and he whipped and sweated adding the salt of his body to the recommended seasoning of the recipes. The kitchen took on the look of a mortuary. Strange mounds and protuberances jutted under white sheets on top of the kitchen cupboards.

Bees buzzed in the golden shower which tumbled in an orange waterfall over the kitchen windows. A fly blundered in and Simeon broke off from his whipping to splatter it against the wall with the palm of his hand. Then he wiped his hand on his apron, picked his nose and resumed his culinary tasks. Charity would later remove the corpse, wash Simeon's apron, and wipe the wall.

Shamba leaned on the fence of the vegetable garden and watched the boys work. He still had problems with the animals nibbling Memsahib's hearty lettuces. Not during the day when the boys were there and the deer remained in the shade of the forest. Shamba decided to speak to Bwana.

Ursula set aside her list to make Susan's party dress. In Nairobi, Ursula had bought fine white imported poplin. The dress was to be created in the style which Ursula would have worn herself when she was a child. So many hours of sewing for a dress that would only be worn once.

Susan took the fitting very seriously. She stood still with arms outstretched to avoid the pins and looked at her reflection in the mirror.

'Susan is angel,' said Ayah and Ursula was pleased. The sun had bleached her hair so that it was fairer than ever but her skin was browner than her mother could have wished, Ursula sighed and blamed her husband. George didn't care how much Susan ran about in the sun.

George meanwhile was working out the quantity of cattle feed required until the rains came and the grass grew. It would be costly. He thought too of the orders his wife had sent out for Susan's party. Perhaps so much expense was to be expected, Ursula knew best.

Simeon worried about his new wife Soya, the daughter of Ayah's friend, who was drafted in to relieve Charity of the washing up while the family was augmented by visitors. The girl stood at the kitchen sink. It was the first time she had been inside the house and seen her husband at work. She wore one of Ayah's old work dresses gathered around her tiny waist by a frayed apron. She had no shoes, Simeon and Ayah felt it was not worth the expense for a few days when no one was likely to notice the girl.

Simeon hovered, enormous, behind her. Soya rubbed her forehead and tried to remember which was the hot tap and which was the cold. One was red and one was blue. One stood on the right hand side of the sink, the other on the left. She touched the gleaming chrome with one finger and looked nervously at the steamy patch it left. If she touched the wrong tap, what would her husband say?

She reached for the tap with the lovely red circle and cold water poured out. She heaved a sigh of relief and held her hand in the stream of sparkling water. Suddenly it turned hot. It scalded her hand and she cried out in pain.

Simeon was amazed that washing up could appear so complicated. Yet it was pleasant to have the child around the kitchen and very distracting. He put a hand on her shoulder to comfort her. His fingers slid like plump sausages over her skinny buttocks. Ayah saw Simeon and Soya as she passed by the kitchen window to hang out the washing and felt that her domestic arrangements were working well. In the evenings she went home to find all the work done and her nights were only interrupted by the baby.

Susan and Isaac ran across the lawn towards the lake. Ayah followed slowly picking up the clothes they scattered in a trail over the grass. She did not like the heat, it made her head ache. The children raced splashing into the water.

'It's cold,' squealed Susan holding her breath, her hands clasped to her chest. Isaac kicked and wriggled his toes into the mud. He scooped up handfuls of water and watched it trickle through his fingers. He threw some at his mother who muttered crossly.

Susan ran along the water's edge, a white gleam followed by silver ripples. Isaac followed, the colour of shade and of the mud stirred up by Susan's feet. They ran until they overbalanced and fell, Susan face down in the mud and Isaac on top of her. But Ayah was there. She lifted Susan, thick with mud and screaming.

'Ayah. Wash it off me. I don't like it.'

Ursula was not on the verandah as usual. She wandered restlessly from room to room followed by Charity. Charity thought the bedrooms looked perfect but knew that she could not rely on her own judgement in such matters. A bed must be moved an inch that way, a pillow smoothed, a spray of bougainvillea tilted to a slightly different angle, until even Memsahib said there was nothing more to do.

Still Ursula moved restlessly about, long after the expected time of arrival of her friend. Her friend, in the arms of the hotel manager, had lost all sense of time, while her ayah and chauffeur exploited the situation to the full. They gorged themselves on huge orders of food and drink, then sat, weighted to their chairs, while the three children ran riot chasing lizards over the rocks and disturbing the other guests.

The chauffeur was on his sixth bottle of beer when Stephanie appeared. She glared at the carnage on the table and then at her servants but they returned her stare and she dared say nothing.

Stephanie silently led the way to the car. The chauffeur, joking and laughing, steered an erratic course along the dirt roads. Fortunately, they met no other vehicles, and the animals had the sense to leap into the scrub at the side of the road as the car approached.

Stephanie began to wonder whether she shouldn't have sat in the back seat rather than the front. Perhaps it would have been better in spite of the shrieking, excited children. The chauffeur glanced often at Memsahib's knees. He was tempted to touch them but was not quite drunk enough. He wondered what it would be like to go to bed with Memsahib and Stephanie pulled her skirt hem lower to cover more of her legs.

On the front steps Ursula stood waiting to receive her guests. Charity stood behind her, Shamba hurried from the garden to carry luggage. The car doors opened and Stephanie's children swept past Ursula without seeming to notice that she was there.

Stephanie got out more slowly and the friends kissed on both cheeks then looked at one another warily. They went indoors leaving the servants in a chattering bunch to sort out themselves and the luggage.

Charity remembered the chauffeur from his previous visit. Seeing him now in his uniform and peaked cap, expertly lighting a cigarette, she regretted having allowed Shamba to move into her room.

'You hurry with cases,' she snapped at him.

♦

On the verandah, Ursula anticipated the usual ecstatic comments on the green lawn and colourful flowerbeds and the beauty of the snow-capped mountain beyond, just discernible in the evening light.

'Who on earth is Susan playing with?' was all Stephanie said. Beyond the demure form of Ayah sitting on the grass in white apron and hat were two naked children. Ursula suddenly saw that one was black and the other white.

'There are limits you know,' murmured her friend.

Ursula thought of the hotel manager and the cucumber sandwiches that she had told the servants to eat up. She supposed that was different, Isaac without his clothes could be any village boy. She did not know what to say, it should be something clever and cutting but the right words wouldn't come. She would have liked to run down the garden and take Isaac in her arms but the moment passed in indecision.

Now Stephanie's children raced into view. They yelled with delight and flung their clothes off as they ran. Soon five naked children were churning up the mud beneath the water.

'That,' thought Ursula, 'will make things better.' But Isaac only appeared blacker by contrast, a dark shade among the porcelain skins.

The children jumped and splashed. They scooped handfuls of mud and squeezed until it oozed between their fingers and plopped back into the lake. The ayahs chatted and watched, and soon chatted and ceased to watch. There was so much to talk about.

Simeon carried out on a tray the best silver teapot and the best china set on a cloth delicately embroidered by Ursula. He bowed and studied his memsahib's friend and was surprised. The chauffeur (ensconsed in the kitchen with Charity and Simeon's new wife) was evidently right. This memsahib was an exotic bird who sparkled and attracted in a manner quite unlike his own memsahib's.

George soon joined the ladies, dusty in his work clothes. The cups were very small after a day in the heat and he drank several. Ursula rang for more hot water. Stephanie, who had begun to wilt, revived and preened herself. George looked like some hero from a western movie, sweat-stained and manly. She was glad that she had come.

'You don't know how lucky you are,' she said to Ursula.

'It's a peaceful spot,' said George and grunted with satisfaction.

'You mean it was peaceful,' remarked Ursula. She watched the shrieking children and wondered if it had been wise to invite such an invasion.

'We have such problems in the city, you can't imagine,' said Stephanie, 'all due to incompetence and mismanagement, Stephen says. It's since all this Kenyanisation of jobs. They simply can't cope. There keep being power cuts, for instance, because of a shortage of water to drive the turbines and the dams are all silted up.'

'My generator might be noisy and smelly but at least it's under my control.'

Stephanie leaned back and lit a cigarette. She stretched her legs and her skirt slid up above her knees.

It's going to be wonderful here. No shortages, no worries. I even had to stop the children swimming in town. The water in the pool looked so peculiar I was afraid it wasn't safe. But this is beautiful, Ursula.'

Ursula nodded, perched on her chair anticipating trouble. The children were slithering down the bank and into the water like otters. Mud was being splattered everywhere and it would be difficult to tell when the game stopped being fun and became a real battle.

What Ursula saw was Susan throwing mud at Isaac, who laughed. Then he threw a handful back at Susan who ducked and the dark sticky mess burst against the cheek of Naomi, Stephanie's youngest child, Susan's friend. Naomi cried with shock and tried to brush it off. Instead she smeared it in ever wider circles.

'Why did you do that?' asked her seven-year-old brother.

'It was an accident,' said Susan.

Matthew picked up a handful of mud and flung it hard. Isaac turned and it hit him on the bottom. Everyone laughed but Isaac had been hurt. He returned fire, missed, and hit Susan in the middle of the back. She was taken by surprise and rushed at Isaac screaming with anger. The others joined in. Isaac retaliated in earnest now and his aim was better than that of the white children. Outnumbered four to one he defended himself any way he could.

The ayahs stood up and shouted. Ursula stood up too, wanting Isaac to come to her so she could defend him. The ayahs kept on shouting but the children took no notice. The ayahs could not enter the water, they had their uniform and their dignity to consider.

It was George who intervened, he strode down the verandah steps, over the grass and into the water. It was easier to get hold of one child than four, so he grabbed Isaac by the arm and pulled him onto the bank. The mud had stopped flying but Isaac was still screaming and kicking George's shins.

'Take him home and keep him there,' he said. 'I don't want to see him in the house again.'

Isaac crept past the verandah naked, clutching his tiny bundle of clothes. Ursula longed to comfort him. If only Stephanie weren't there. As Isaac's bare back receded round the corner of the house, she thought perhaps Stephanie was right after all. Without clothes he did look just like one of the gardening boys.

Ursula sipped her tea but a sick feeling gripped her stomach. She thought she could hear Isaac crying and wondered what they were doing to him. But she sat without moving while Stephanie and George discussed milk shortages and meat shortages and the vagaries of servants.

'Are you feeling all right?' asked George once. 'You look a bit pale.'

Speckled with brown like new-laid eggs, the white children had a hot bath.

'You shouldn't play with servants' children,' said James.

'Why not?' asked Susan.

'My mother said.'

'Why?'

'Because they're dirty.'

Susan wondered how Isaac could be dirty. He bathed and changed his clothes as often as she did but however much he was scrubbed he stayed the same colour. Perhaps James was right.

'Why is he black?'

'Because he's a Kenyan.'

'I'm Kenyan and I'm not black.'

'You are silly,' said Matthew. He was seven and knew everything. 'He's black because his parents are black.'

'If Ayah was my mother,' thought Susan, 'I'd be black.' She sometimes wished Ayah really was her mother but was not sure if she wanted to be black like Isaac.

'If I had a white father and a black mother would I be striped like a zebra?'

'No,' snorted Matthew. 'You'd be sort of brown, like coffee. Like some of those children at school.'

Isaac was in his room. It was dark because his mother had bolted the door on the outside. He sat on the edge of the bed and picked the mud from his skin. Now it was dry it was like picking a scab. He forgot his anger and grief, absorbed in what he was doing.

Susan's fourth birthday dawned with the same intensity as the day of her birth. The sun rose with a dreadful inevitability and only the children awoke with their usual energy and enthusiasm. Stephanie sipped tea on the verandah and wondered how on earth she would get through the day. Ursula drank her tea in bed, cup after cup, and wondered if it was worth the trouble of having a shower when she would instantly be sticky again.

While Matthew, James and Naomi scampered barefoot down the garden after Susan, their ayah was regaling Susan's ayah with tales of town life. They sat on the back doorstep with a pot of tea between them. Ayah was envious. Stephanie's ayah seemed to have absorbed something of the sparkle of her memsahib. She wondered if the same thing could be said of her. She heard tell of a world where the washing was done by machine.

'Look, my hands,' said her friend by way of advertisement. Ayah studied her own, rough and chapped by frequent immersion in detergent. Her friend's hands were still not quite like a memsahib's but they were an improvement. She admired the length of the nails and their varnish.

Susan raced down the garden anticipating the 'Happy Birthday' that would ring on everyone's lips.

'It's my birthday,' she carolled to the shamba boys as she flew past. They stopped work and smiled.

'It's my birthday,' she sang to Shamba.

'Very good, Memsahib Susan,' he said as he swept up the jacaranda pods for fear they would damage the lawnmower.

'It's my birthday,' she whispered to Simeon as he snipped the rind from her father's bacon.

'Many happy returns of the day, Memsahib Kidogo,' he whispered back.

'It's my birthday,' she shouted to her father as he padded down the corridor towards the bathroom in his pyjamas.

'Happy birthday,' he shouted back then caught her up and threw her into the air as high as a bird and the movement matched her feelings.

After breakfast the family and the ayahs gathered on the verandah. Charity lingered as she cleared the table. From the corridor, Simeon peered across the living room and through the open doors leading onto the verandah.

First came the biggest present from her parents. A shiny red bicycle with stabilisers fitted onto the back wheel. Susan sat on it smiling stiffly while George took her photograph. Then came the party dress, no surprise to Susan after all the fittings but an opportunity for the adults to look and admire.

From Stephanie and the children there were crayons, a doll and a jigsaw puzzle. Susan settled down with the puzzle while Matthew, James and Naomi went off with the bike. They took turns to ride down the path, once round the septic tank and then back.

Isaac, lurking in the bushes, saw the bike as if in a vision. He could not imagine anything more wonderful. For several rounds he just watched before the idea of riding the bike began to grow in his mind.

'Please can I have a go?' he asked as Matthew pedalled by on his fifth turn. Matthew didn't turn his head.

'Please can I have a go?' asked Isaac more loudly on the next circuit, perhaps Matthew hadn't heard him the last time. Still there was no answer. The next time, Isaac stepped out in front of Matthew blocking the path.

'Please . . . '

'Get out of my way,' yelled the white boy. Isaac stood aside. But he tried once again.

'Please can I have a go on the bicycle?' This time he stood his ground and Matthew rode the bike hard at him. The front mudguard dug into Isaac's shin. He stepped into the bushes and wiped the blood from his leg with his hand, then he picked up a stone.

It was Naomi who cycled past next, so Isaac waited. As Matthew came by, Isaac flung the stone and hit him between the shoulders. Isaac ducked as Matthew turned round so that he couldn't be seen. On the next circuit Matthew rounded the corner flanked by his troops.

'You threw a stone at me.'

'You hurt my leg.'

'Well, get out of my way next time.'

'I want to ride the bike.'

'Black boys don't ride bikes.'

Matthew rode straight at Isaac who grabbed the handlebars. Isaac was far too small to knock him off. Crying with frustration he sank his teeth into Matthew's wrist. James and Naomi ran towards the house to tell their mother.

'That damn toto of yours,' shouted Stephanie. She never liked being disturbed.

Ursula ran down the garden, outraged at the sight of Isaac being pummelled by the bigger boy. But the big boy was white and a guest. She sent Isaac back to his room for his own protection. What else could she do? She locked the bike in the outhouse. Matthew was too big for it anyway.

♦

'Where is Susan?' asked her mother.

Nobody answered. The table was laid and the guests were seated.

'Has anyone seen Susan?'

'You can't have an éclair. Not yet.' Stephanie slapped her daughter's hand as she reached out. Naomi howled.

'I said, has anyone seen Susan?'

'I'll go and look for her,' said George. He scraped his chair backwards on the stone floor and stalked off.

They were having the party on the verandah where everyone could benefit from the slight breeze, and the view, and the crumbs wouldn't matter.

Susan's ayah tried to distract Naomi's attention from her stinging hand but Naomi was hungry and wouldn't be comforted. James and Matthew kicked one another under the table and giggled.

'Thank goodness I'm going home tomorrow,' thought Stephanie.

'Tea?' Ursula spoke loudly and held the pot high above her head in case her friend could not catch her words above the noise. She also wanted her friend to notice her mother's best silver teapot. Stephanie nodded. Although she disliked clutter she was not immune to the occasional pang of envy.

'She's not indoors,' said George.

'Have you tried the toilet?'

'Of course I have.'

'Ayah, where is Susan?'

'I think she with you, Memsahib.'

'Well, she isn't, is she?'

'I go see, Memsahib.' Ayah trotted down the verandah steps and out into the garden.

'Perhaps Susan has gone to visit Isaac,' said Ursula, pleased to think he wouldn't feel so left out. 'I think we may as well start tea. It's not fair to keep the other children waiting any longer.'

James and Matthew dived for the nearest plate of cakes.

'Sandwiches first,' said Stephanie, whisking the plate up out of the boys' way. She sipped her tea and felt too hot to eat anything herself.

'You have nice sandwich,' Matthew's ayah said to him. Naomi already had an éclair crammed into her mouth and was stretching for another.

Susan's ayah was worried. Susan didn't seem to be in the garden or the servants' quarters. She would search the house in case Bwana had missed her. He didn't know about their game.

'Susan,' called Ayah through the nursery door, and listened to the emptiness.

Then she had an inspiration. Suddenly she knew where she would find her.

'Susan, I'm coming to get you,' she sang.

'Is Susan under the bed?' she questioned, crouching low.

'Is Susan in the laundry basket?' She took off the lid. 'Pooh. It too smelly for Susan in there.' Ayah strained her ears for the sound of a giggle.

'Is Susan behind the chair?' Ayah began to panic.

'Susan. Game is finish. I come get you now.' Ayah flung the cupboard door wide open and felt along the wall, behind the racks of dresses and the unworn coats. There were no shoes with legs in them.

CHAPTER 11

'I think you should have waited for her,' said George. 'After all it's her party.'

'In that case she shouldn't have wandered off. She knows it's tea time.'

'She's only four!'

'So long as she comes in time for the cake. That's what really matters,' laughed Stephanie, embarrassed.

'Want some cake,' chanted Naomi.

'I'll blow out the candles for her,' offered James.

'We won't light the candles until she arrives,' said George.

Ayah returned, her face screwed up against the sunlight, or perhaps with anxiety. From far away came the noise of the lawnmower. Birds were singing.

'Memsahib, I not find Susan.'

'Bother the child.'

'Why don't we all look?' suggested George.

'Let's not break up the party. The ayahs can go. And Charity and Simeon.'

'Quite right,' said Stephanie. 'It wouldn't be fair on the other children. She's caused enough trouble already.'

'Go and look in the garden,' Ursula ordered the servants.

'But Memsahib, I think Susan with you, putting on her party dress.'

'She was, half an hour ago.'

The servants walked away. The plates of sandwiches were nearly empty.

'I'll save some for Susan,' said George. He put two small crustless triangles of bread filled with egg and banana onto Susan's plate, then one of each sort of cake as well.

'She'll never eat all that.'

'It's her party.'

'Mind if I smoke?' Stephanie smiled, thinking it was typical of men to spoil their daughters.

'Well, I'm going to look for Susan,' muttered George.

Ursula and Stephanie exchanged glances.

'Just like a man,' said Stephanie. 'If *we* panicked like that we'd be on our feet all day.'

'Let the ayahs earn their keep for a change,' agreed Ursula, then snapped 'Don't do that!' at Matthew. Matthew froze, a large lump of icing off the side of the birthday cake half-way towards his mouth.

'You can't blame them,' said Stephanie. 'We've all waited long enough for your daughter.'

The two women seemed scarcely to notice when the children left the table and went into the nursery to play with the gifts they had given Susan earlier in the day and so they missed the tableau that took place on the lawn below the verandah.

From the left, at some distance, entered a procession of servants, the two ayahs, Charity, Simeon, Shamba and the chauffeur. Approaching slowly from the opposite wing came George. No one spoke. Their feet made no sound on the grass. The birds, disturbed, were silent.

Stephanie paused as she lit another cigarette, her thumb on the flint of her lighter. Ursula saw the two groups meet and stop as if a film had suddenly jammed.

'Oh God!' Stephanie screamed, and jumped to her feet. The cameras started rolling again. Air returned to Ursula's lungs though she did not move. George took the white bundle from Ayah and stumbled towards the house, up the verandah steps, past his wife. Ursula saw a white dress streaked with mud and water dripping, dripping over the verandah floor, leaving a small dark stream in the carpet of crumbs.

The door of George's study slammed. Ursula looked at the box of matches, crumpled in her hand.

'The floor cloth, Charity,' she said.

From the lawn came a long low shriek, the sound of an animal in pain. Ursula shivered. It was not the kind of sound a human should make. She must take command of the situation, banish the nightmare.

'Stop that noise,' she shouted and clasped her hands over her ears.

'I do not want to intrude on your sorrow,' said Stephanie, and was gone in half an hour. Her ayah packed for the children, flinging clothes higgledy-piggledy into the suitcases. She grabbed some of Susan's dresses in her haste but it didn't matter since Susan wouldn't need them again. She added a couple of Ursula's necklaces as well.

Towards the end of the drive Stephanie realised that Naomi was clutching the doll she had given Susan for her birthday. Stephanie felt it was unlucky to have brought it with them. She tried to grab the doll and wrestled with her daughter on the back seat.

Opening the car window Stephanie hurled the doll as far as she could. It flew limply in a high arc, its limbs dangling grotesquely, and was swallowed up in the bushes. Naomi screamed, then whimpered for her lost treasure until she fell asleep.

Ursula knocked on the study door but received no answer. She tried the handle but the door was locked. Ayah was slumped in the corridor, her head on her knees, her arms round her legs, apparently neither seeing nor hearing.

Ursula turned away from Ayah and went back onto the verandah. She instructed Simeon and Charity on how to clear the table. They scuttled around casting frightened glances in her direction, trying hard to do well and make up in some way.

'What I do with cake?' asked Simeon. His beautiful cake like a fairy castle, with an unlit candle on each of its four turrets.

'Put it in the freezer,' said Ursula, counting her mother's silver teaspoons. At some stage the notions of certificates and officialdom filtered through Ursula's brain. She rang for the doctor. She sent for Isaac and watched him gorge himself on the leftovers until he ran down the garden to be sick.

The doctor gained access to the study through the open window and then unlocked the door. He scattered conventional crumbs of comfort which bobbed away on the surface of George's misery and left something 'to help Ursula sleep'.

Ursula took her draught and retired to bed. What else could be done? George perched on the arm of the couch, next to Susan's head, with a bottle of whisky. Ayah crept in and sat on the floor at Susan's feet. George and Ayah, like Father and Mother, as they once had been over her cradle.

Twice Simeon came and shook Ayah's shoulder, for her daughter cried with hunger. Ayah felt the pressure of milk in her breasts and welcomed a physical location to her pain.

George sank into a whisky-laden sleep. While he slept Ayah got up and scrubbed Susan's room until it was as immaculate as on the day of her birth. She tidied away clothes and toys and opened the windows wide to let in the cool dark air.

She washed and ironed the beautiful party dress though there was one patch of green slime which would not come out.

She sponged mud from the pale skin and washed and brushed the golden hair.

Then Ayah kept vigil alone, cross-legged by the bed, and felt her bowels being slowly turned and wrenched inside her.

Angel Susan. White.
On the white bed
In the white dress
In the white room.
Like the gleam of snows on the mountain
The unearthly whiteness of the home of the gods.
Jealous gods
Who had called her name.
She should have had no name
Not yet.
To draw attention to her perfection.
Beauty that would never walk the earth again
For her humble servant.

George awoke with the dawn and staggered down the corridor. A sense of loss gnawed at him, a pain that was all he had left and he feared its diminishing.

Instinct led him towards the nursery, to a white world of cold sunlight where creepers overhanging the window swayed like reeds and green shadows danced. Here light and shade chased over the still, white figure. 'Surely she moves?' George prayed. He gripped the bed rail until his knuckles turned white, the only restless spirit in the room. For Ayah sat, calm now, solid and dark, smooth and rounded, glowing like the pebble on a river bed, sun-soaked and heavy.

Ursula awoke with a feeling akin to a hangover. Charity brought a tray of tea and drew the curtains back. Ursula saw the sun shining as usual and sipped her drink wondering where George had spent the night.

In slippers and dressing gown Ursula wandered down the

garden and saw the sun slant through the lime-yellow branches. Zebra stripes skittered on the grass. In the hollow of leaves beads of dew were cradled like jewels. The world was created anew, resonant with birdsong.

Shamba unbolted his door and came out yawning and stretching. He saw Memsahib wander down the garden.

'Today I not water. I not cut grass. I not weed.' What a wonderful day lay ahead. Memsahib had said so, out of respect. He slapped Charity on the bottom as she dashed from the kitchen across to the toilet. She came back and washed her feet.

'I hope Memsahib not spoil dressing gown,' she said. Such a beautiful dressing gown, she dreamed that one day it might be hers.

Ayah had left George alone in the nursery. She sat on the doorstep of her room dazzled by the clarity of the morning. Her skin and throat and eyes felt hot and dry. So did her breasts. Her daughter still cried though Ayah had nothing more to give her.

Simeon stumbled towards the kitchen shielding his eyes from the light. While his fellow servants ate their maize meal, the smell of frying bacon wafted glorious through the open back door.

His first wife, Wambui, was packing. Today she would take Ayah's voracious daughter away back to that village to the south of Nairobi from which she had returned to help at the birth. Here the baby would be fostered by Simeon's second wife, Mumbi, who had never set eyes on her husband's other home.

Isaac dressed and urged his mother to hurry.

'I'm hungry,' he wailed.

Still Ayah sat on the doorstep, watching the pink blur that was Memsahib moving through the trees.

'If I Memsahib,' she thought, 'I not get up today.'

Memsahib reached the end of the garden and looked out over the plains, at the bones of the starved animals. Impala stared at her before bounding away.

George left the nursery and began looking for his wife. All was quiet apart from the sizzling of bacon. Ursula was not in bed. He realised that he should have thought of her before,

Susan's mother. He stomped down the corridor yelling for tea.

'And find Memsahib,' he added.

The tea had already been made and drunk by Simeon and Charity. They giggled and topped up the pot as Bwana's footsteps came nearer. Simeon bellowed out of the back door.

'You boys, go find Memsahib.' He did not want to go himself, nor did Charity. They had their clean white shoes to consider but the shamba boys ran barefoot through the dew. They had few clothes and the sun would warm them.

Ursula returned slowly. Her feet were wet and cold and the hem of her dressing gown dragged behind her. At a respectful distance followed the two boys with pot bellies and huge dark eyes.

'Stop following me,' snapped Ursula and they bounded into the bushes like startled animals.

Back in her bedroom Ursula slipped out of her muddy dressing gown and slippers and sat on the edge of her bed. Charity brought more tea, and toast wrapped in a serviette to keep it warm. There was a saucer of butter curls and a new jar of marmalade.

Charity on her way to the nursery with a tray of food, nearly collided with George who came out of the shower, rubbing his hair with a towel. George was surprised at the sight of so much food on the tray and no Susan to feed. Somewhere between the bathroom door and the nursery two eggs and several pieces of toast vanished into Charity's apron pocket.

Charity left Isaac eating, watched by Ayah at the nursery table, and skipped down the garden heedless of her white shoes – for Shamba.

Ursula finished her breakfast and went into the nursery. George stood silent at the bedside. Ursula was gratified by the beauty of her child, tumble-washed and spun, bleached of her sun tan. She suddenly glimpsed the relationship they might have had if only she had been more like this in life.

Ursula was overwhelmed by a sudden feeling of loss, of opportunity missed. She stood with her head raised, unseeing through her tears.

George, sensitive to the sudden swell of emotion in his wife moved closer and put his arms round her.

Ayah watched through the open door, turned and crept away. Where could she find comfort?

Shamba sat on a rock in the early morning sun, ate and counted his blessings. He had acquired the look of a sleek, well-fed cat. His skin shone and his legs had filled out. He wore new clothes, donated by Bwana, and took care not to dirty them.

While he ate, the shamba boys planted out tiny seedlings that would flourish in the rains. Their roots would delve deep into the soil before the next spell of hot dry weather. The boys smelled the toast after their five-mile walk to work on empty stomachs. In ten years' time they knew one of them might sit where Shamba now sat, eating toast dressed like a white man. Promotion, Shamba often reminded them, was only achieved through diligence.

When he had finished eating, Shamba licked the crumbs from his fingers, dusted his clothes and put on what he hoped was a funereal expression. He had been detailed to open car doors for the mourners after the funeral.

Ursula took the candles off the cake. On second thoughts she replaced them, for disguise was impossible. As far as she could see, there were four possible answers to the problem of 'what to do with the cake'. She could have offered it to Stephanie for Naomi's birthday, although it was doubtful whether it would have been accepted. She could have kept it in the freezer until Isaac's next birthday. This answer lay nearest to Ursula's heart but George would not approve. At the reception after the funeral which was, after all, to commemorate Susan, the cake could make a poignant centrepiece – the crowning glory of Simeon's efforts for the day.

Ursula turned and saw Muriel in the doorway. From Muriel's expression, she realised that not everyone would approve of her decision to use the cake up in this way. Hence the fourth alternative. Ursula picked up the cake and handed it to the priest.

'For the poor,' she said.

CHAPTER 12

As Ayah pegged Susan's dresses out to dry on a line slung between the lime tree and an avocado, she aired a few more memories – Memsahib sewing, Susan playing and laughing, the weight of Susan heavy with sleep on her shoulder. Most precious, was the thought of Susan running barefoot down the verandah steps in the early morning, cheeks still pink with sleep, as she flung her arms round her ayah's neck.

Ayah cleaned the nursery every day and arranged flowers as in a shrine. Susan's fingerprints were gone from the walls and windowpanes. Isaac was not allowed in the room any more, his mother forbade it.

Charity saw Susan's dresses hang limp and lifeless in the sun. She cast her mind back to the white figure she had seen on the afternoon of the party, tracing patterns in the water with a stick. Charity had been cleaning windows beneath the birds' nests in the eaves. How she hated those birds but Memsahib liked to see them flutter around the house.

Charity had sat with her back to the lake, her bottom balanced on the window ledge as she leaned out. When she turned round, the child was gone. There was not a sound, not a ripple, only the calm surface of the water. She missed the child who had followed her about, like a sunbeam in the darkest corners of the house, playing at housework.

'My daughter,' thought Charity, 'my daughter would never have let anything happen to Susan. My daughter who has no husband though I would gladly reduce the bride price. She keeps the hearth for no man, and I sleep with Shamba who was once wife of Simeon.'

'Perhaps,' suggested George, 'we should think of having another child?' He watched Ursula, who sat with Isaac on her knee.

'I said, perhaps we should have another baby?'

Ursula was in the middle of a story. George walked over to her chair and took away the book.

'Run away and play,' he said to Isaac. Isaac put his arms tightly round Ursula's neck and giggled.

'My memsahib,' he said and hid his face against her cheek.

George grabbed Isaac under the arms and propelled him towards the verandah steps.

'Go and help your father,' he shouted.

Isaac was confused. Bwana sent him down the garden to help his father, when all the time his father was in the kitchen, his father with the huge white apron. His father was an important man and loved him, not like Bwana.

'I want another baby,' said George. 'I can't bear this.'

'You shouldn't have done that, in the middle of a story.' Ursula picked up her embroidery and George could not see her face any more.

'Is that all you can say?'

'With you in that mood, yes.'

Isaac wandered about the lawn collecting seed pods to put in his pocket, only he had no pocket. He slipped them in the waistband of his shorts and they fell out at the leg. Isaac didn't notice. With bent back, he continued is gleaning.

Shamba saw Isaac. He turned off the mower and crept closer from tree trunk to tree trunk, silent among the shadows. He rushed out at the child on hands and knees, growling.

Isaac screamed and ran towards the house. Shamba was hurt, he had only wanted to play.

'I too have lost a child,' he thought. 'My son, child of the passion-flower vine, conceived darkly. And I loved his mother, a gazelle with thighs of polished ebony and laughter a birdsong on her lips.'

Isaac clambered through the shrubbery and peered between the verandah railings. There was no sign of Bwana so he pulled himself up onto the banister and leapt onto the concrete floor.

'Did you see that, Memsahib? Did you see me? I flew!'

Ursula had walked onto the verandah just as Isaac launched himself into the air. She laughed with relief as he stood up, chattering.

'Your lip's bleeding,' she said. She gently dabbed at the wound with her white handkerchief then showed him the stain. How red was Isaac's blood!

Charity bustled onto the verandah complaining about people's dirty feet ruining her cleaning.

'Well, fetch a cloth,' said Memsahib.

Ayah's baby daughter had now reached Simeon's village on Wambui's back. They had been given a cool reception and the child was fed grudgingly after Simeon's second wife's baby had had first suck. It was only natural that Mumbi's own child should come first.

The women laughed to see how like her father the baby girl already was, and her mother a Masai. Aie. It was amazing. She bore no resemblance to her half sister but then Simeon was only at home for two weeks in the year.

Ayah's daughter soon ceased to be fat and ugly, but she was never to become a beauty.

'How is the farm?' Ursula asked over supper.

George looked up, surprised.

'I didn't know you were interested.'

Ursula stabbed a piece of meat and chewed. And chewed.

'This meat isn't properly cooked.'

'Oh? I like it like this.'

Ursula picked out the mushrooms and tomatoes and piled the meat on one side of her plate.

'I think I'll have some more,' and George held out his plate.

'Help yourself.' Ursula pushed the casserole over.

'I'm sorry I was cross this morning,' said George.

Ursula shrugged and mopped up gravy.

'At least Simeon can make good bread.'

'Ursula, please will you think about what I said?'

'Yes. I'll think about it.' She rang the bell for Charity.

After supper Ursula packed Susan's dresses into a cardboard box.

'What are you doing with them?'

'Sending them to the orphanage.'

'But we might have another daughter.'

'How macabre you are, George.'

Ayah came in with another pile, lovingly ironed.

'Where is the pink one?'

'Pink, Memsahib?'

'Yes, you know the one, with lace round the collar.'

Ayah's heart sank. She wanted to keep one dress, just that one, Susan's favourite, hanging in the cupboard where they played their hiding game.

'Please, Memsahib, I keep.'

'They must all go.'

'Memsahib, please.'

'No.'

So Ayah brought the little dress. Her hands shook at the thought of black children wearing it, dirty, unwashed, unwanted children, squatting in the dirt.

'Damn it woman, let her have it if she wants it.' George snatched the dress from his wife. 'Here, take it and go.'

On the following morning, George stood in the shower and

listened to the sounds from the nursery.

Isaac arrived before his mother these days, now there was no Susan to greet her. He laid the table and carried the milk jug into the kitchen for Simeon to fill. On the way he peeped through Memsahib's door to see her lying under the white lace bedspread with her dark hair fanned out on the pillow.

He heard Bwana open the bathroom door and ran, grinning shyly over his shoulder.

'He's not such a bad little fellow, perhaps he'll help her get over it,' thought George.

Simeon was frying bacon gently and evenly. It never stuck to the pan. When Bwana closed the bathroom door after his shower, Simeon added fried bread. When Bwana walked down the corridor with shoes on, it was time for the fried eggs. Isaac stood by his father's elbow, crunching bacon rind and admiring his skill.

Ayah smelt the bacon and heard Simeon sing as he worked. She wondered how life could appear so normal as she sat alone at the nursery table.

George heard Isaac's thin high voice pipe a monologue down the corridor towards the nursery in the wake of the breakfast tray, but there was no Susan to cuddle her father and murmur, 'Did you have a nice sleep, Daddy?' With dripping hair and a towel round his waist, George flung open the nursery door. There sat Isaac, guzzling toast and marmalade, watched by Ayah, in a play that had lost its meaning since the central character was missing.

'It's time you found another job,' said George into the silence. 'There is no work for you here any more.'

Ayah saw the huge white expanse of Bwana's bare chest and thought of the small white body like a crescent moon turning over and over in the water's gentle flow. She dreamt without hope of bearing Bwana's child, a pale foetus in the dark waters of her womb. Her daughter, with golden hair.

'Yes Bwana,' she whispered and pushed aside her plate. Ayah walked into the garden and sat on a stone with her face lifted towards the sun. She felt its warmth soak into her skin and flow down her throat. She remembered Memsahib Stephanie glistening with oil, the air around her saturated with perfume and a curl of smoke from the ashtray by her hand.

'I don't know why I should work my fingers to the bone feeding unnecessary servants – and their children.'

'Oh,' replied Ursula who had not envisaged Susan's death having such repercussions. She had assumed Ayah would continue to come and look after Isaac which was, she now saw, nonsensical. Mothers are not employed to care for their own offspring.

'If we had another baby there might be some reason for keeping her.' The thought had occurred to George in the shower.

'But I don't want another baby?'

'Then she must go.'

'Not yet, anyway,' added Ursula.

Ayah went to Memsahib's desk and helped herself to writing paper, an envelope and a stamp.

'Please you help me find job,' she wrote to her friend, Stephanie's ayah. 'I come any time. Here is no work for me.' She asked Bwana for Memsahib Stephanie's address which Simeon wrote on the envelope in block letters. But how did one post a letter?

Charity said a letter had to be put in a letter box. Ayah found a red one in one of Susan's picture books but they all agreed that they had never seen anything like that in the area. Simeon thought he had seen one once on his way through Nairobi on a bus.

'You ask Bwana,' he said. Twice a week Bwana drove off and returned with letters and newspapers. Ayah lay in wait one day as Bwana reversed the truck from the garage.

'Please Bwana, I go with you?' she asked.

'Hop in,' he replied, swinging open the door.

'Ever been in a car before?' asked George. Ayah clutched the edge of her seat and closed her eyes as the world flew past, she felt the wind in her hair, a magic breeze since there was none outside.

'Are you shopping?'

'I post letter.'

'I'll do that for you, just put it in the pile.'

Mindful of Memsahib's envelope and stamp, Ayah hid her letter at the bottom of the pile. She tried to imagine the small rectangle of paper arriving in her friend's hands, but could not.

Ursula sat on the verandah making dresses for the orphanage out of coarse local cotton. The colours were cheerful in a crude way but the material was strong and it would last. She imagined rows of little girls with black curly hair marching in crocodile, with white veils held on by a narrow strip of elastic, just as she had worn at school.

The weather was heavy with the scent of roses like June in the south of England, the feast of Corpus Christi. Since dawn the girls would have been in the garden gathering rose petals. The sun always seemed to shine on her childhood in Somerset where the girls saved their pennies to buy black babies. For two and sixpence they could have a baby of their very own.

The forms to be filled in were printed on the back of black and white photographs of small, dark, serious children in European dress. At sixpence a week that meant five weeks until the child was hers, a little doll with fuzzy nylon hair, and huge eyes. Five weeks per baby, two and two-fifth babies per term, over five years that made thirty-six babies in all. There might have been one or two more since Ursula always gave up sweets during Lent.

Once upon a time Ursula had cherished pictures of her growing family. Such wonderful names she had given them, thumbing through the obscure names at the back of her missal: Philomena, Etheldreda, Ezekiel, Dagobert. They had to be saints' names for the baptism.

Ursula felt as though thirty-five years on she was making dresses for those same children. Her extended family who, the nuns said, used to arrive naked and never having slept in a bed before. Now they were all Christians.

'Memsahib, please, you make me new dress?' asked Ayah on her return from the post. She had seen such lovely materials at the store. Ursula laughed and continued her sewing. She had forgotten that all her little Christians had grown up and still needed clothes.

Ayah looked at her Memsahib. How drab she was! There was no sparkle about her. Memsahib Stephanie had heels that clicked and skirts that swirled, lace-trimmed petticoats and a transparent nightdress.

'Memsahib, Bwana say I find job.'

Ursula squinted towards the sun, threaded her needle and poked it in and out of the harsh material.

'Memsahib, Bwana say I not work here any more.'

Ursula thought of the advertisements in the paper under Situations Vacant or For Sale. It would be so much easier to find a home for a cat or a dog. She pricked her finger.

'Can't you see I'm busy?'

'Sorry, Memsahib.' Ayah went to do Isaac's washing. Then she picked fresh flowers for Susan's bedroom.

Isaac crept up behind Ursula and suddenly put his hands over her eyes.

'Guess who?' The hands were dark and salty.

'Good morning, Isaac,' laughed Ursula. Isaac rubbed his face hard against her back like an affectionate cat.

'My memsahib, what shall we do today?'

Ursula laid aside her work. Now Isaac was four she thought often and seriously about his education. She consulted books that said he needed company and stimulation. The only children available were locals and she could hardly invite the children of white neighbours to come and play with the son of a servant. Stimulation was possible however, he must not just play.

'Today, we shall paint,' she said.

'Let me help. Let me do it,' Isaac begged as she stirred water into the coloured powder.

'When you are bigger,' she replied. Ursula mixed turquoise and pink, lilac and eggshell blue, the colours she favoured in her own clothes and jewellery. The weak colours did not show up well on the white paper.

Isaac drew the paintbrush over his dark skin. He laughed and his white teeth flashed, the pale colours glowed. He spread paint further up his arm and little rivers of colour dribbled onto his clothes.

'Watch me,' said Ursula. She took the brush and painted a pastel house and pastel person. Isaac smeared paint onto his sheet of paper with a brush in each hand, until there was no white visible. The bristles splayed and the paper disintegrated. It was not what Ursula envisaged. Ayah laughed and Ursula left.

Charity had washed the servants' uniforms in the soapy water left over from Bwana and Memsahib's underwear. She hung them on the washing line to be crisped and baked, then she joined the painting party.

'I paint?' Ayah handed Charity a brush and some paper. Charity touched the pure white paper with the tip of her brush and drew back alarmed by the monstrous blemish. She dipped her brush again and again until the whole sheet was transformed into a lilac mass.

Simeon tiptoed enormously across the grass casting furtive glances behind him. He looked at the sky, then nonchalantly down at the paint. Ayah held out a brush but he shook his head. He would not try his hand, not before an audience.

Shamba had fewer inhibitions and not much to do. He tried every colour and proudly carried away the resulting patchwork to hang on his wall.

Only the shamba boys did not try. They watched eagerly but no one thought to offer them a turn.

Ayah mixed more paint. She spooned in powder and added water drop by drop. She did not mix pastel shades, her colours were deep and violent, the red, purple and vermilion of bougainvillea, the scarlet of the desert rose and electric blue of the agapanthus, the rich brown red of the soil.

Isaac began to paint in earnest, the colours bright against the paper. At first these were just experimental splodges but then came people with matchstick arms and with legs sticking out from their heads. Then he began adding an indeterminate number of eyes, tummy buttons and penises. Simeon laughed, Charity put her hand over her mouth and sniggered. Shamba clutched his stomach and bellowed. Only Memsahib made no comment.

The walls in the servants' room sprang to life. Purple cars and green smiling faces hid the bare bricks. Strange animals wandered through prehistoric groves. Ursula wondered at the quantity of paint and paper Isaac used. The painting sessions had moved deeper among the trees, out of sight of the house. Sometimes there were not enough brushes for Isaac to have one and he spent the morning messing about in the stream.

Ursula put the extravagance in art materials under the heading of Education, but about her ball of string and sellotape she was not so sanguine. She looked in her desk, on the dressing table and in her workbasket. She stormed into the kitchen and found Simeon and Charity drinking tea side by side on the back doorstep. Breakfast things still cluttered the sink. A mountain of beef was defrosting over the kitchen cupboard, enough to feed a regiment rather than make hungarian goulash for two.

Charity and Simeon leapt to their feet and grinned, looking foolish. Memsahib dealt with the situation with deadly calm.

'If the string and sellotape do not appear within ten minutes, there will be trouble.'

Shamba who had been just round the corner, out of sight, melted away into the shrubbery. Within minutes Charity was being propelled down the corridor with Simeon's large hand in the small of her back. She poked her head out of the verandah door then a shove from behind catapulted her into view.

Memsahib sat watching and held out her hand.

'Where were they?'

'Oh Memsahib, the sellotape she slip down behind the settee.'

Memsahib reflected that the settee had used an awful lot of sellotape. There was hardly enough left for her parcel.

'And the string?'

'Oh Memsahib, Isaac she take down garden.'

Memsahib swept into the kitchen and took Simeon out to the shed where the freezer was kept. She was surprised to find that she and George, with a little help from Isaac, had devoured one whole beef cattle in about four months. She locked the shed and put the key in her pocket.

'In future, I will remove the meat for thawing, every day after breakfast.'

Simeon was appalled at the prospect of a diet of maize meal and scraps but the alternative of buying his own meat was even more horrific. Memsahib would relent sooner or later.

One tea time, George returned from the post carrying one of Stephanie's scented envelopes. Even his newspaper was tainted.

Ayah held the letter reverently in her hands. She had never received a letter before. It seemed like magic. She went into the kitchen to share the opening ceremony with Charity and Simeon.

'Memsahib Stephanie, she have lovely paper,' said Ayah. She smoothed it with her fingers and compared it with her memsahib's rough plain sheets.

'Read it,' begged Charity.

'I read,' said Simeon, taking it from Ayah's hand. After all, he was the cook. First he had to go to his room and fetch his glasses, bought from a secondhand shop on his way through town.

'I HOPE YOU WELL. I AM. I AM HAPPY TO GET LETTER. I HOPE YOU COME. IS BETTER YOU COME STAY WITH ME. THEN YOU FIND JOB. VERY NICE JOB. FIRST COME.'

There was no indication who the letter came from but Ayah knew.

'I go now,' she said.

Not quite now, but a few days later, after breakfast, George got out the car. Simeon, empty-handed, led the procession of his wife's belongings carried by Charity, Shamba and Simeon's new wife, Soya. Kettles and saucepans jangled together. The bottoms of numerous cardboard boxes sagged. Brilliantly coloured kitengis were knotted Dick Whittington style over mysterious lumps. George piled everything onto the back seat and into the boot.

'Is that all?' he asked.

Shamba and Charity reappeared round the corner of the house with a chest of drawers and a bed. George opened the other garage doors and reversed the pick-up into the yard. Patiently he transferred all the luggage and wondered how much more might appear from the one small room.

At last the truck was loaded. George climbed in and put his keys in the ignition. Ayah climbed up beside him and slammed the door. Simeon, Charity and Shamba began waving.

'What about Isaac?' George looked at his watch and turned off the engine.

'Isaac?' Ayah looked puzzled.

'Yes, Isaac.'

'He stay, Memsahib.'

George dismounted and headed towards the house. He had been cheated. The child must go. He would not have him there without his mother.

'Ursula,' yelled George. He stamped from room to room flinging open doors onto total silence.

At the furthest end of the garden, Ursula strolled with Isaac out of earshot of the house. She imagined that George might have assumed that Isaac was going but she had not actually misled him in any way. She had simply left him to form his own conclusions. Ayah had never spoken of taking Isaac with her, just as Ursula had never spoken of him going.

Isaac was squatting down engrossed in watching a large white slug. He stretched his hand towards it and laughed.

'See,' said Ursula. 'He has pulled his horns in.'

They kept very still until the tiny protrusions reappeared and lengthened and the slug continued on its way until Isaac stuck out his hand again. It was a good game.

'Did you know, Isaac, that in Africa the slugs are white and the people are black? In England it is the other way round.' She wondered whether it would be safe to return to the house.

'I would like to stay with this slug for ever and ever,' said Isaac. So they stayed, to be on the safe side.

George looked again at his watch and swore. He kicked a pot of geraniums and knew he was defeated. The car accelerated violently away, shooting gravel at the waving servants and drowning their messages of farewell in a sound like rifle fire.

Shamba fetched a rake to repair the damage to the drive. Simeon stood still and watched until the truck was out of sight. There was no point in waving because of the mushroom-shaped cloud of dust billowing behind the car. Ayah would not be able to see him.

Ayah was nervous. She had never been to town and never driven so fast before. Bwana scowled at the road and said nothing. He drove fast and furious thinking of Susan and his unborn children and Ursula at home with Isaac on her knee. The whole journey passed in silence. Ayah was happy alone with her dreams. She was excited and felt that her life would begin anew.

'I need a drink,' said George as Stephanie greeted him at the door and offered her cheek.

George sat on the sofa and swallowed three whiskies in quick succession. Stephanie sat close beside him, so warm and feminine, so understanding. She didn't say much, just made soft noises in her throat like a mother hen. She held George's hand and re-filled his glass each time it emptied.

Stephanie felt sorry for George. He needed a child, especially after all he had been through. She could not understand Ursula's rejection of him, but then she had always rather fancied George herself. Stephanie also felt outraged on behalf of the whole white community over Ursula's attachment to the little black boy. She had let them all down. She had forgotten to 'keep her distance'.

George wept and Stephanie took him in her arms to comfort him, like a child. Ayah at the living-room door, come to report that the trunk was unloaded. She saw Memsahib Stephanie's face over Bwana's shoulder. Memsahib scowled and Ayah retreated and closed the door with a stab of jealousy in her heart. Afterwards she was sorry that Bwana never said good-bye.

The rest of George's afternoon was befuddled by whisky and guilt and a warmth he had never known before. He slept his first real sleep since Susan's death a month previously. For twelve hours he lay on the settee. Stephanie covered him with blankets and guarded the living-room door.

At dawn, when the house was still quiet, George woke and headed for home. He arrived at mid-morning to find Ursula and Isaac sitting by the lake. Ursula had a box of watercolours on the grass next to her.

'Why do you always sit here?' George shuddered.

'Why not?'

George looked at the ducks and saw them dive. On the far side of the water a malachite kingfisher shimmered like some pantomime Tinkerbell. It felt peaceful and safe, as if Susan's ghost had been exorcised.

'Why not?' he said and smiled.

George sat on the grass next to his wife and Simeon brought a glass of iced beer.

'Bwana is hungry?'

'I'll wait until lunch thank you.'

Ursula was surprised that George should choose to sit with them, and slightly irritated. She felt that she ought to make conversation though the mood of the place was for silence.

'Did you have a good journey?'

'It was too late to come back last night.'

Ursula watched Isaac's body merge into the shadows and cool brown water. If she closed her eyes she had to look hard for a few minutes before she could find him again. She wondered how to capture that feeling on paper.

'How is Stephanie?'

'Much as usual.'

'The children?'

'I didn't see them.'

'Not even last night?'

'No. I drank too much and then I fell asleep.' George had

not wanted to see Naomi, Susan's friend. George leaned over to look at Ursula's painting and was surprised by the beauty and softness with which she painted the child. Perhaps he had been wrong to expect her to part with Isaac. But how could he know when she expected him to divine all her thoughts and feelings without any real communication between them? Perhaps he should try harder.

'That's lovely,' was all he said.

Ursula recoiled from a sudden wave of Stephanie's perfume unmistakable and sickly.

'And how is the hotel manager?' she asked, smiling.

'I didn't inquire.'

Ursula on a pedestal, absorbed the knowledge of George's fallability and decided she ought to feel shocked. Mother would have been. Instead she felt a certain amused satisfaction.

'Simeon,' said Ursula later in the day, 'now that Ayah is gone Isaac should move into the nursery. I will look after him.'

'Oh yes, Memsahib.'

'I expect your wife will be busy with her own child before long.'

'Oh yes, Memsahib. Thank you, Memsahib.' Simeon was relieved. Ayah had said that Memsahib would care for the child. He had hoped it would happen sooner, rather than later. Why should he be burdened with Isaac who was not even his child?

His monstrous daughter now, was different. But she lay on a heap of stinking rags hundreds of miles away. Old Wambui was weary from trudging to the well for water to spoon down the child's throat or to wash away the liquid faeces. But she loved the baby. She sang to her and held her close, easing her passage towards death.

When George returned from checking his cattle, Ursula was tucking Isaac up in the little white bed. Susan's bed. He looked so black against the white sheets but George felt the dark stain on his own soul and said nothing. He headed for the whisky bottle. It was empty.

'Simeon,' he roared. 'You're fired!'

Simeon waddled into the room behind his enormous starched belly. Bwana brandished the empty bottle in front of him like a tennis racket.

'Bwana,' said Simeon with great dignity, 'I no drink. I good Christian.' Very slowly, with great ceremony, Simeon took off his hat and placed it on the dining table. He folded his apron over the back of a chair.

'I go now, Bwana. I have signed pledge at Mission. When I was little boy.' He indicated his size as about knee high. In the doorway he turned.

'Please to tell Memsahib, dinner is in offen.'

Charity served dinner after Memsahib had emerged flushed from thickening gravy over a hot stove and whipping cream to spread on the mousse. The cream was served separately in a bowl and not piped in extravagant swirls as usual.

'I really think,' she said, 'that you might have spared his feelings.'

'Damn his feelings. What about my whisky?'

'If you are going to treat the servants in this way, it will be impossible for me to keep the household going.'

'But the man's a thief!'

'They all are. You shouldn't leave your whisky lying around like that.'

'It wasn't lying around. It was in the cupboard.'

'Well, keep it locked.'

'I'm not going round with a bunch of keys like a jailer.'

'It's what most people do.'

'I am not most people.'

'Simeon is a good cook and I don't want to lose him.'

After a silent dinner, George went soft-soled to knock on Simeon's door. He carried a bottle of whisky which Simeon accepted with a show of disdain. No words were exchanged but next morning the smell of burning bacon filled the house.

CHAPTER 13

The first drops of rain fell silently and vanished into the dusty soil. Ursula, sitting on the verandah in the late afternoon, wondered whether she had imagined them. Dark blotches remained, staining the concrete. She shivered as a sudden chilly breeze dispersed the sticky closeness of the air.

Charity ran to the washing line and returned under a mountainous pile of washing, scattering a trail of clothes pegs across the grass.

Shamba turned the mower towards the garden shed. He turned off the motor and there was a thick, heavy silence.

At the back door Simeon graciously accepted a basket of artichokes brought at a run by one of Shamba's boys.

A window banged, then the breeze dropped. Birds flew to roost and trees hung limp, waiting. Heavy globules of rain burst on the dead ground, each drop slow and ponderous, like syrup.

Ursula moved her chair to the back of the verandah against the house wall. Charity ran from room to room fastening windows.

The deluge exploded with a thundering intensity that isolated the house within opaque barriers of water. Lightning cracked and the water fell with a steady roar.

Ursula hugged Isaac close to her and pulled a rug around them. Isaac fought against the heavy, prickly material. He wanted to see what was going on but Ursula was afraid. It was as if she were under water, cold unfriendly water that washed away banks and uprooted trees and swept everything before it.

George was drenched but the last fence post had been driven home. He hurried lest the track degenerate into a sea of mud before he reached the house. Not that he was alone. He had his men in the back of the truck. There would be plenty of hands to push if necessary.

The rain had its own peculiar smell, at once repellent and seductive. Water that destroyed but also released the goodness lying dormant in the soil.

Shamba shivered in the doorway of the hut. He could do no work in the garden but Memsahib said that he had to be at his post, within call of the house in case he was required.

Dusk arrived and still no one moved. They watched the rain and inhaled the dampness into dust-choked lungs. Charity opened a window and leaned out laughing to feel water drum on her palm. Ursula took off her slipper and put a bare foot onto the railing. She felt the stab of the water, cold and sharp.

'I want to go out.' Isaac squirmed and wriggled until Ursula went into the nursery and took out one of Susan's unworn macs, a sou'wester and wellington boots.

Isaac, dressed all in scarlet, ran laughing down the verandah steps into the wall of water. He held out his arms and stamped his feet to feel the grass like sponge beneath him.

From their underground nests great waves of white ants floundered into the air like overweight dragonflies. They flapped about blindly till they collided and fell to earth in writhing, mating heaps. Then, shedding their wings, they scurried in pairs, nose to tail, in search of shelter beneath the tree roots.

Isaac caught them, pulled off their wings and crammed them still wriggling into his mouth. Rain trickled down inside his collar and sleeves as he capered about with upstretched arms, the insects whirling like a snowstorm about his head.

In a frenzy of excitement Isaac peeled off his coat, shorts, shirt, socks and boots which were by now as wet inside as outside. He stood naked except for his scarlet hat and laughed as the rain scourged his body. He lifted his face towards the sky, eyes closed against the fierce lashing and let the water flow into his mouth.

Ursula ran to prepare a hot bath in case Isaac should catch cold and she laid out clean warm clothes, since the night would be chilly.

Isaac took to Simeon a hat full of ants. Simeon fried them in butter and added a light seasoning of pepper and salt. Still Memsahib could not eat them. She would have liked to because Isaac had taken such trouble collecting them but somehow she could not put them in her mouth.

George returned home cold, tired and stiff to find Isaac sitting in the bath merrily letting the hot water gurgle down the plug hole. He shouted for Charity to light a fire, but there were no logs.

Shamba was sent to chop firewood. An hour later he went home cold and shivering to a room where there was no fire and no hot bath. He should have remembered that logs would be needed every evening during the rains.

Ursula sat watching the unaccustomed greyness of rain become the greyness of dusk.

'Why are you sitting here in the dark?' asked George and turned on the lights. Now Ursula could see nothing but the glisten of nearby rain, and ants, like moths, tapping gently against the window panes. Some squeezed under the door, blind and sluggish, as they lumbered towards the open fire.

George sat by the fire with his cup of coffee, his wife on the opposite side of the fender – an idyllic picture of family life by one of the old Flemish masters. Ursula stitched and felt the fire glow warm on her face and legs.

But George felt restless. He opened his newspaper and turned to the cricket. He would have liked to share the excitement of England's last innings with his wife but knew she would not be interested. He stuffed the paper into the bin and went to ring his friend Bill.

In the morning the paper would be carefully salvaged, the crumpled pages smoothed and restored to their correct order. Simeon, as head of the household, would read it during his lunch hour. In the sun, with his back against the whitewashed wall, Simeon would search for accidents and calamities. Foreign news did not concern him nor did local politics unless related to domestic servants. On such issues, he negotiated with Memsahib on behalf of all the staff.

Ursula never failed to point out that she observed all regulations to the letter. Also that she made none of the deductions she was entitled to – for housing or electricity. Sometimes she looked at her diminishing sacks of flour, rice and tea and was astounded by her own generosity.

Simeon read with interest the news that two American women tourists had been gored by buffalo while on safari.

Charity received the newspaper in the evening. She deciphered the print by paraffin lamp in her room. Insects sizzled against the hot glass, some she swotted onto the table, others she splattered against the wall. Frequently she paused to wipe her hands on her dress or to rub her stinging eyes.

Shamba listened intently while he pored over the pictures – overturned vehicles, dismembered bodies, a policeman with smoking revolver standing over a supposed criminal, a row of corpses large and small laid out along some dusty roadside. White people looked grey, black people looked black but the soles of their feet showed up white. Shamba looked at his own soles and was proud of their pinkness.

In the next room Simeon, Ayah and Soya had the benefit of a charity performance of the day before the day before yesterday's news. The dividing wall between the rooms stopped at the level of the eaves.

Charity traced each line with her forefinger. She hesitated, sounding out some words and guessing wildly at others. Simeon sometimes helped out, suggesting words over the partition, or bellowed with laughter over some of her interpretations. They shared their reading as they shared everything in the circumstances. They had more privacy than they would have in their own villages, Memsahib was quick to point out to her friends.

The newspapers read by so many, still had their uses as toilet paper, draught stoppers, bed covers, wall paper, or to prevent Memsahib's underwear from snagging on a chance splinter in her dressing-table drawer.

The fire in the living room spat and crackled. A globule of resin bubbled through the bark of a pine log and burst into a blue flame. Ursula looked into the heart of the fire. As each branch became charred and too brittle to hold its shape, it crumbled into red hot ash and the picture changed.

George returned from the phone flushed and excited after re-living the match that had taken place on the opposite side of the world. He thought of the day when he might enjoy such an event with his son, just as he had done with his father. Afternoons on the village green with a seat outside the pub. Peering through the leaves of the horse-chestnut tree, large as dinner plates, at a local team who could never play as well as the spectators. Perhaps it was only once or twice, it seemed like always.

George poured himself a drink and paced up and down the room. He turned on the radio. On the other side of the valley, Bill could listen to the test match live. George twiddled the knobs, waggled the aerial. He finally picked up and shook the set, cursing the surrounding hills. The voice of the commentator remained an unintelligible drone beneath a counterpoint of static. He turned up the volume and counted the overs missed. Did he hear cheering or was it merely interference?

Ursula left the room and went to bed, hoping to be asleep before George arrived. George abandoned the cricket, turned on the centre light in the bedroom, which never failed to annoy Ursula, and crashed in and out of the bathroom.

'Not asleep already, are you?' George looked suspiciously at his wife huddled under the bedclothes. He climbed into bed and ran his fingers along her iron back. He became bolder. His hands wandered over her shoulders and hips. He pulled her towards him and saw her wet cheeks.

'Oh God. I'm sorry,' he said and got up to fetch another whisky. He tried to imagine what Ursula must still be suffering. After all, she was Susan's mother.

CHAPTER 14

The harsh croak of bullfrogs was replaced by the nightly jar of crickets. Ursula was pleased with her garden, the leaves still clear of dust and as fresh as early summer in England, the flowerbeds a riot of colour. Shamba developed a new pride in his work. Earth which had caked and dried in a solid crust was broken and smoothed by his rake. The grass grew smooth and even, after regular trimming with the rotary blade of the mower.

Now he hated to see the shamba boys skimp their tasks. They did not take the trouble to weed properly but skimmed the surface of the soil with their pangas leaving the roots untouched. He followed them, nagging.

By ten o'clock it was very hot; too hot to spend another four hours crouched in the herbaceous borders. The boys watched jealously while Shamba polished the mower and adjusted the sprinklers on the lawn.

Charity suggested the lads might be offered a cup of tea. Shamba agreed reluctantly that they could join in the morning and afternoon tea breaks provided that they did not expect to share the back doorstep or take too long.

The boys had never tasted tea before. They found it bitter unless it was made syrupy with sugar. Then they looked at one another and beamed at their good fortune. But they kept quiet, it was not for them to engage in conversation with their elders.

The return of warmth to the sun brought a feeling of spring. Memsahib looked at her servants and ordered new uniforms by post.

For Simeon came a dazzling white coat, apron and hat. In a fit of generosity Memsahib also ordered trousers since Simeon was too large to squeeze into any of Bwana's.

Charity received an orange dress and headscarf and a white

apron. The dress was made of the cheapest local cotton. When new, it was stiff and uncomfortable, when washed it shrank and the hem sagged.

Shamba was disgruntled at receiving nothing new, only a pair of old trousers and a couple of shirts slightly frayed at the collar. Anyone with an eye for quality would have realised that Shamba had the best deal of all; he saw only that Memsahib had not considered it worth spending any money on him. He felt devalued. Even the shamba boys were resplendent in new T-shirts and shorts with zips that worked so that Memsahib's gaze was not offended.

George kicked a row of toy cars out of his way and sat down with a magazine. He found it hard to concentrate with all the noise. Isaac had heaped all the sofa cushions onto the floor and was diving onto them from the window sill.

'Look mummy, I can fly!'

'Be careful, Isaac.' Ursula looked up from her sewing and laughed.

'I can fly. I can fly.' Isaac launched himself into space with his arms flapping wildly. George winced and shrank deeper into his chair. Isaac landed with a thud.

'Shall I put more wood on the fire, Bwana?'

George did not answer.

'You are a kind boy, Isaac. But be careful. Don't get too close.'

Isaac picked up a large log and threw it into the fire. He laughed to see the red hot wood crumble under its weight. George stamped angrily on the ashes smouldering on the hearth rug.

'I do think you should answer the child when he speaks to you, George.'

George grunted and hid behind his article on new methods of dealing with the tsetse fly. He felt at a disadvantage because of the letter that burned in his pocket. His wife had already sniffed it out and read it while he was in the shower. She had suspected something when her bank statement arrived smelling of perfume, but no letter for her from Stephanie.

George was in agony. Stephanie said that she was expecting

his child and George did not doubt her. She had hoped to miscarry but now she was nearly four months pregnant and wondered whether George and Ursula might like to adopt the child?

Ursula watched George, wondering what he would do or say. He poured himself a whisky and wondered how to begin. She calculated the chances of Stephanie becoming pregnant from one act of intercourse with her husband and decided it was very unlikely. She wanted to ask George how he enjoyed making love to Stephanie. She would have liked to ask Stephanie what she thought of George. The minutes ticked by while Isaac went on jumping and shrieking and George drank and Ursula waited.

'Bed time, Isaac!' called Ursula.

'I'll tell her when she comes back,' thought George. 'When Isaac's in bed and it's more peaceful.'

'She cannot stay here indefinitely,' Stephanie told her ayah.

'No, Memsahib.'

'I counted the number of people in the yard this evening. There were fifteen.'

'Yes, Memsahib.'

At the club today Stephanie had decided it was the last time she would be able to wear her bikini until after the baby. She mourned already for the warmth of the sun on her slim stomach.

'Eight adults and seven children in three rooms!' Her voice became shriller.

'Yes, Memsahib.'

'And only four of them work here.' She wondered whether George would phone, soon, before Stephen returned from work.

'Memsahib, she cross?' asked Ayah. 'Is better I take job with your friend.' The room was small and the pay less than she had hoped for in the city.

'Yes, is better you take.'

Ayah went to Memsahib Stephanie who was walking in the

garden smoking. A gentle breeze blew Stephanie's dress against her body and moulded the material to the soft outline of her expanding womb.

'Memsahib have baby in the tummy?' asked Ayah, hand over mouth, giggling.

Stephanie stopped walking. She stood with her back to Ayah. 'Do you want something?'

'Memsahib, when you say you have baby?'

'December.'

Ayah was reckoning in her mind and on her fingers. She thought back to her arrival in Nairobi, to the scene she had witnessed between Stephanie and George. Oh it should not have been Susan's father. Then she thought again – if only she were Stephanie.

'Memsahib, I have job.'

'That's good.'

'I not like that memsahib but children are nice.' Ayah scratched her head under her headscarf and wrinkled up her face.

'Oh? Where are you going?'

'To Memsahib Gillian.'

'Well, good luck then.' Stephanie half-wished she could keep Ayah for herself, she was so good with children, especially with babies. But she felt there was no justification for having two ayahs, not with the older children at school. Anyway, Stephen would never agree.

Stephanie went into the house, poured a sherry and hovered over the telephone. She picked up the receiver and started to dial George's number. She did not know what she was going to say. She heard Stephen's footsteps in the hall and changed her mind. She dialled Gillian's number instead.

'Gillian, it's me, Stephanie. I'm ringing about your new ayah, the one that's starting work tomorrow . . . Of course I know her, she used to work for Ursula . . . That's right, yes, wasn't it terrible? I thought you ought to know . . . Oh dear, I suppose you're right, but it seems a pity . . . Yes, quite, I would feel the same . . . What's that you said? . . . Oh, the baby, yes it was a shock, I thought those days were over . . . Yes, Stephen's thrilled. He wouldn't mind how many we had . . . Don't worry I'll tell her. Cheers for now.'

Stephanie sent a message to say that Memsahib Gillian did not require an ayah after all.

Ursula was gone for a long time. George paced up and down with his drink. He looked into the nursery where Ursula still sat on the bed reading to Isaac.

'. . . but the higher they flew, the more slippery did the glass become. They could scarcely hold it. They flew on higher and higher, till at last the mirror trembled so fearfully that it slipped from their hands and fell to the earth breaking into millions, billions and trillions of pieces. Some people were so unfortunate as to receive a little splinter into their hearts – that was terrible! The heart became cold and hard like a lump of ice.'

Ursula felt George in the doorway though she did not look up. Isaac lay with his thumb in his mouth, eyes half-closed.

'The Snow Queen was very beautiful, he could not imagine a more intelligent or lovely face . . . In his eyes she was perfect.'

George leant against the doorpost and closed his eyes. Ursula moved to stand up but Isaac flung his arms around her neck and wouldn't let go.

'The Snow Queen kissed little Kay and he no longer felt the intense cold all around.' Ursula closed the book.

'Mummy, stay here,' murmured Isaac. 'Don't go.'

Ursula bowed her head and rested it on Isaac's chest until his arms went limp and she could disentangle herself. She straightened the white bedspread smooth under the dark chin and tiptoed from the room.

'Ursula . . .' George began.

'I know.'

They leant next to one another on the rail of the darkening verandah. Colour was fast fading into a grey-green darkness. George did not ask how she knew, he felt only relief. He moved to put an arm around his wife's shoulders to draw her closer to him but she stepped out of reach.

'What shall I do?'

'It's her problem, not yours.'

'But it's my child.'

'With the sort of life she leads, she should know better than to get herself pregnant.'

'It was my fault.'

'It could equally well be the hotel manager's.'

'It's mine. She said so and I believe her. Ursula, I want the child to live with us.'

'And make us a laughing stock?'

'I don't care what other people say.'

'But you have to care. Think of people like Bill and Muriel.'

'It wouldn't bother them.'

'Well, what about the Smiths and the Wetheralls, and all the rest of them. Imagine going to the Club and all of them knowing . . .'

'But Stephen thinks the child is his.'

'Yes, and you should leave well alone. You'll only cause problems.'

Isaac stirred and cried out. Ursula turned to go to him but George stood in her way.

'Isaac needs me.' George stood, a black shape between her and the child, and for a moment Ursula feared defeat.

'So do I,' said George. He stood aside then strode into the garden. Through the nursery window Ursula saw the pale glow of his shirt among the trees. She stroked Isaac's tight curls and he was soon quiet again.

Ursula made up her bed in the spare nursery bedroom. From her own room she brought armfuls of clothes, her make-up, perfume and hairbrush. Soon her half of the wardrobe was empty, and her nightdress gone from under the pillow.

George saw the stripped room and felt justly punished for his sin. He sat on the narrow white bed.

'Ursula, don't leave me. Please.'

'Don't be so melodramatic, George. I'm simply moving here to be nearer to Isaac. He may be sickening for something.'

George sat quietly while Ursula tidied her things away; handkerchiefs and tights in neat piles in the top drawer; pants, petticoats and nightdresses in the second. The screw of one handle protruded slightly into the inside of the second drawer. Ursula frowned and hoped it wouldn't do any damage. She placed her face cream and hand cream on top of the cupboard.

Then she went into the bathroom. George waited until she came back in her nightdress and sat on the white stool. He watched as she brushed her hair. He saw the reflection of her face in the mirror, the eyes clear and untroubled.

Ursula got into bed and switched off the bedside light. George stood up and walked out. As Ursula fell asleep, she heard the car starting up.

CHAPTER 15

The next morning Simeon stood next to the cooker with three rashers of bacon (minus rind) spread on the chopping board. He waited for the sound of Bwana going for his shower, for the slam of the door and the clonk of hot water through copper pipes.

'Bwana, she gone?' asked Shamba. He had found the garage doors open and the car gone. The boys had already raked over the tracks left by the tyres to restore the gravel to its former neatness.

Charity sang down the corridor where the sun cast latticed shadows over the tray of tea she carried. Such a lovely day! She knocked on the bedroom door. She waited and knocked again. She put her ear to the wood and felt the emptiness on the other side. No longer singing, she turned the handle and saw that the bed had not been slept in, that Memsahib's dressing table was empty.

In town Ayah did not sleep well. She had lain awake and worried or slept fitfully, awakening with nightmares that left her sweating and trembling. She crept out of bed early to make tea for her friend before she had to start work. Ayah sat in the warm sun with her hands cupped around her drink and sipped thoughtfully.

A policeman wandered slowly up Memsahib Stephanie's drive. His revolver slapped against his thigh. The night watchman with his rusty panga followed closely. It was as well to be careful, not all policemen were genuine.

The policeman rang the doorbell but there was no reply. The house was large and the servants were not yet on duty.

'Is better we find housegirl,' said the askari.

In the yard there was only Ayah, still sitting on the doorstep. She called her friend, who woke the chauffeur who woke the housegirl, with whom he was sleeping, who woke Bwana.

Stephen came to the door in his dressing gown and came face to face with a short fat man in grey shorts with socks hanging round his ankles. He had had a late night. He rubbed his knuckles into his eyes and blinked. The dark moon face looked up at him with a wide, crescent grin.

'Well?' said Stephen.

'Bwana, I have news for you.' The policeman waved a grimy document. 'Bad news,' he added.

'What is it?' Stephen imagined the office safe rifled or his servants involved in a drunken brawl.

'Your friend is dead, George Patterson.'

'You'd better come in.'

They passed Stephanie in the hall fluttering like a moth in her nightdress, drawn towards the scene.

The policeman left, the children woke and the servants arrived. Stephen rang the office to say he would not be in, there seemed to be so many formalities connected with George's death.

'You'd better go and tell Ursula,' Stephen said.

'In my condition?' wailed Stephanie. She rang Muriel and gave her the job.

Stephen took his wife back to bed and made love to her. Stephanie had read somewhere that the contractions of the uterus in orgasm could lead the womb into premature labour. She lay and thought of George, now dead, and of Ursula who had never seemed more than half-alive. She wanted to be rid of the child and pretended a passion that made her feel further and further away from any climax. Then her thoughts moved on to George alive and on his way to see her, even dying for her. She wondered what might have happened had he lived. Her excitement increased and she felt that George's baby was the most wonderful thing in the world. She cried out in pleasure and gasped at the sudden contraction of her womb and feared that George's seed would be lost for ever.

When Isaac got up he saw the shape of a body under the white covers of the spare bedroom. He peeped through the door and saw his mummy's hair dark, like a gleaming waterfall over the pillow. He crept closer and put his little black hand on her shoulder.

'Mummy,' he whispered.

Ursula drew back a corner of the bedclothes and pulled the child in beside her.

'Your feet are cold,' she said, cupping them with her hands. Isaac snuggled closer. He did not dare go into the bedroom when Bwana was there. Secure and warm he drifted into sleep again until Charity brought the tea.

It was Ursula who now prepared breakfast at the nursery table for herself and Isaac. Just the two of them. She asked Simeon to make something special for the occasion, waffles perhaps. She ate her cornflakes while Isaac chattered excitedly.

'Where is Bwana?' he asked once. Ursula shrugged. With that whore she imagined, and wondered what would happen next.

'What shall we do today, Mummy?'

'What about a picnic?'

Ursula rang the bell for Charity, who groaned at having to walk as far as the nursery. The dining room was nearer the kitchen. Ursula ordered a packed lunch. Simeon put away the packet of bacon and buttered rolls instead, marmite for Isaac, crab and mayonnaise for Memsahib. The shamba boys waited for the smell of frying bacon to drift into the garden. They wondered what was wrong.

Memsahib folded the picnic rug neatly at the bottom of her basket. She took some knitting, and a book for Isaac.

'Shall we take these?' asked Isaac, bringing a handful of cars and his teddy bear. Ursula was trying to persuade him not to take them all when a car stopped outside the house and Ursula's heart sank.

'That will be Daddy,' she said, though Isaac never called George 'Daddy'. She wondered whether she would have to cancel the picnic for fear of upsetting her husband or whether to go ahead with their plan. After all, he was the one who had walked out. She did not even turn her head at the knock on the door.

Ayah peered through high white gates towards a building that resembled a fairytale palace, white and dazzling in the sun. The house was larger than any she had yet seen. Shambas were sweeping lawns as smooth as the baize of a bridge table, others plucked imaginary weeds from the ornamental flower urns lining the immaculate driveway.

Inside the building, among the marble corridors, Ayah soon began to feel like a shadow. She neither washed nor cleaned – her function was simply to drift in the wake of the two little daughters of the house with their kohl-blackened eyes. Giggling, they gave her occasional orders, but mostly they ignored her.

Ayah came to dread the memsahib's shrill nasal whine which was liable to erupt without warning. The memsahib and the servants went barefoot in the house, silent and all in white, like ghosts.

On her first day off Ayah went to Memsahib Stephanie's and drank in the human warmth – the teasing and laughing, the endless cups of tea. At the end of the day she could not face going back to the silence and coldness, so she stayed with her friend and learned of the arrangements Stephanie had made for George's funeral.

'Won't you stay with us?' Stephanie had asked Ursula.

'A hotel would be better, I think. I would like to be on my own.' Ursula could not contemplate leaving Isaac with the servants, nor could she take him to Stephanie's.

'I'll book you a room,' said her friend, relieved, and wondered how much Ursula knew.

'What I do now?' Ayah asked her friend.

'You go home. Memsahib she take after funeral.'

Ayah wondered where 'home' was. It was not the mud hut with her mother and brothers and sisters, nor was it Susan's home any more. Simeon had his new wife and baby.

'Please you tell Memsahib I help with baby.'

'Memsahib say one ayah is enough.'

'Oh.' Ayah was knitting for Stephanie's baby. The needles creaked and groaned for her hands were slippery with sweat. She would have liked to care for Bwana's baby, for another Susan.

'We find you new job,' said her friend.

Administering to bereaved widows was a new experience for Stephen. He had several beers to fortify himself before Ursula's arrival and dreaded being faced with an emotional situation beyond his control. He was surprised to see Ursula climb from the car looking much the same as ever, clutching a small toto by the hand.

Stephen hesitated and waited for someone to materialise and lead the child away, some servant up in Nairobi for a holiday perhaps. Ursula mounted the hotel steps with the child in tow.

'Ursula, my dear!'

'Stephen, how very kind of you.'

'Come and have a drink.'

'Stephen, you must meet my son Isaac. Isaac, shake hands with Mr Ford.'

'Hello Bwana,' said Isaac. Ursula wished he would not grin like that and that he would stop calling white men 'Bwana.'

'Son?' said Stephanie later. She was polishing her nails. She recalled the spiteful little toto who had wounded Matthew.

Perhaps George's death had totally unhinged Ursula?

'She hasn't adopted him, has she?'

'I didn't ask.'

'She can't have adopted him. He's black.'

Ursula and Isaac shared a room on the ground floor. The hotel was built around a quadrangle which contained the main hotel gardens. In the centre was a high, wrought-iron aviary. Isaac stared in wonder at the multi-coloured parrots who cracked nuts and laughed like a bunch of old crones.

'Hello.'

'Did you hear that, Mummy? Did you? He spoke to me. He said "hello".' Isaac pressed his face between the bars and Ursula pulled him back, fearful for his eyes.

'Who's a cheeky boy, then?' asked the parrot. Isaac was convulsed with laughter. He made such a noise that Ursula led him off to the bedroom before he attracted attention.

On the next day Isaac woke before his mother. His eating habits had been disrupted by the journey up to town. He had eaten nothing for his supper but had drunk three bottles of Coca-Cola then wet his bed. Isaac got up, peeled off his sodden pyjamas, then made his way to the bird cage.

The hotel manager, on his way to inspect the kitchens, saw the naked toto with horror. Seizing Isaac by the arm, he called for reinforcements. Isaac clung to the aviary bars and screamed for his mother. Out she rushed in her nightdress.

'There, there. It's all right,' she soothed him. 'No one will hurt you.'

'How was I to know?' asked the manager, quite charming now, all apologies and smiles.

'You see he didn't even have shoes on,' he explained.

In the black car on her way to church, Ursula thought of her father's funeral, and of crows raucous over a countryside heavy with a late-autumn melancholy. Today the sun shone and brilliant materials glowed on dark skins. At the traffic lights a huge red flower plopped onto the car bonnet.

Ursula climbed out of the car into a sea of well-wishers.

'Ursula dear, how marvellous you look.'

Ursula turned to see her friend, elegant in black.

'Stephanie,' said Ursula, eyeing her friend's stomach. 'Why didn't you tell me?'

Stephanie laughed and tossed her head, happy that her secret had been kept.

'Was it a mistake?'

Stephanie stopped laughing.

'I love my children,' she hissed.

Ursula made her triumphant progress up the aisle, shaking hands to right and left. Ayah sat in the back pew feeling faint and hungry. No one sat next to her although the other benches became quite crowded. She had walked a long way in the hot sun, she did not like to ask Memsahib Stephanie for a lift.

Ayah watched Ursula glowing in the gloom, all in white as a sign of faith and hope. 'I am the Resurrection and the Life,' intoned the priest and Ursula hoped for forgiveness for George, dying like that with such a sin on his soul.

Stephanie snuffled into her handkerchief.

'She's always like that at weddings and funerals,' Stephen explained to the person sitting next to him.

Stephanie could not even see the flowers she had sent and wondered if this was Ursula's doing. She glared through her tears at the murderess sitting so piously on her right.

Ayah looked at the pine box with brass handles and tried to imagine Bwana shut up inside. It was impossible. Bwana would not fit into such a small box – Bwana who laughed and shared his sandwiches with his workers, who tossed Susan into the air as though she were a feather. Yet Bwana had shrunk in Ayah's mind since Susan's death to become the figure weeping like a child in the arms of Memsahib Stephanie. And now Memsahib Stephanie was carrying his child.

Ayah looked in disbelief at the silent congregation and was surprised that George's death meant so little to them. Perhaps white people did not have feelings?

'She's staying at the Caledonian,' said the woman in front of Ayah.

'With some toto she calls her son!'

'What's she going to do now?'

'Staying on I gather.'

'But what about the farm?'

'There's a manager there already.'

'It's not her child, is it?'

'Too black for that. But she behaves as if he were . . .'

In the front row Ursula was hardly aware of the service. She was worrying about Isaac in the care of the hotel ayah. She had told him to keep his shoes on and had ordered lunch to be served in the bedroom, sausages and chips. There were swimming trunks and armbands on the dressing table in case he wanted to swim.

'Why won't they play with me?' Isaac was asking the ayah. When he went near the other children they grabbed their towels and rubber rings, flippers and snorkels and glared at him.

'Please may I have a go?' Isaac asked, but they looked the other way ignoring him. When his mummy returned he would ask her to buy him flippers and goggles. He knew she would say yes, but he was lonely. His ayah chatted to the pool attendant in a language he couldn't understand. He sat in the shade watching the other children splash and giggle.

Isaac's mothers, physical and adoptive, were still in church. Ursula bowed her head and thought about her appointment with George's solicitor. She thought about the children begging in the streets and wondered how anyone could object to her becoming Isaac's mother in an official sense.

To one side of the altar Ayah noticed a still figure in a blue dress, with hair like Memsahib's long and loose on her shoulders, and the same distant look and pallid skin. But this memsahib wore a circlet of stars in her hair which flickered in the candlelight.

On her knee, the woman held a child of about two years old. The little girl Ayah would have recognised anywhere, with her bright dark eyes and soft tangle of golden curls. Ayah closed her eyes and felt the words of the robed figure at the altar flow over her, like Bwana reading Susan a bedtime story. She was filled with a terrible ache for those days. She did not cry out loud but wept inwardly, like a white person.

With scraping feet the congregation rose for the final hymn. The organ thundered holy chords until the roof reverberated, then there was an echoing silence and the feet of the coffin-bearers tapping on the flagstones.

Ursula followed the coffin, walking alone, with her eyes on the small bunch of lilies of the valley that jiggled on the slippery wood at each step. Ayah longed to fling herself at Memsahib's feet and beg to be taken back.

The familiar material of Ayah's dress caught Ursula's eye as she passed. She remembered camping with George in the days before Susan was born, a large acacia set against a backdrop of blue mountains, and she felt a pang of regret for the past.

Ayah longed to reach out and catch the hem of Memsahib's dress, to remind her how they had once needed one another. And now she, Ayah, was lost and alone. But the moment passed and Memsahib was gone.

Stephanie followed, red-eyed, and gave Ayah a wan smile. Ayah did not smile back. She did not even see the smile, only the soft bulge shrouded in black that was Bwana's baby. Ayah imagined the flutter of tiny limbs and her womb ached. She knew then that her place was in the city with Bwana's child.

Outside the church, Ursula watched George's coffin slide into the hearse. Only then did she wonder who could have been wearing the dress so similar to one she had worn long ago.

Inside the church Ayah approached the altar fearfully. She had to get nearer. The candles, alight since early morning, were nearly burnt out. Melted wax encrusted the brass candelabra. The fitful light seemed to give life to the two cold figures. It showed up the cracks in the plaster and the finger missing from the woman's right hand and Ayah felt cheated.

But she sat until the last candle guttered and the statue sank into lifelessness. Still the stars gleamed and Ayah sat waiting for the moment when the woman would smile and hand down the child for Ayah to cuddle and love.

She decided to go to the hotel and visit her son.

CHAPTER 16

Ayah walked five miles to the hotel through the dust and the whistles of workmen. Her shoes pinched and her head ached. She halted before the imposing entrance then smiled, reassured by her reflection in the expanse of plate-glass.

The receptionist glanced up from his newspapers as Ayah stood, half-hidden by a rack of postcards. He rang for the doorkeeper who should have been on duty.

'I help you?' The doorkeeper advanced.

'I want see my son.'

'Your son is working here?'

'Oh no.'

'In kitchen perhaps? In shamba?'

'No. He stay in hotel-ly.'

The doorkeeper laughed until the receptionist looked up.

'Is better you go. Meet me later and we have fun, eh?'

'I want see my son,' Ayah insisted.

A man lurched out of the bar.

'This lady is a friend of mine,' he said. He put a hand under Ayah's elbow and steered her into the bar. A glass of gin and bitter lemon appeared before her. The man spooned in ice.

'Have a drink, you'll feel better.'

'You are friend of Bwana's?'

The man nodded and Ayah sipped her drink. She felt the bubbles burst in tiny iced sprays against her nose. The drink slithered cold down her throat and put fire in her stomach. Drink followed drink and the bwana was so kind. He leaned close to catch every word and put an arm round Ayah's shoulders. He understood all her problems. Ayah blew her nose and dabbed her eyes. She knew he could make everything come right in the end, like a fairy godmother.

'Let's go and find your son,' he said. They stumbled past the doorkeeper and the receptionist who tactfully looked the other way. Ayah felt a small glow of triumph. The bwana pushed her in the direction of a lift but she hesitated.

'Never been in one before?'

Ayah shook her head. Laughing, the man pressed a row of buttons. The doors shut. The lift accelerated upwards and Ayah felt as if her insides were being torn out.

'When I go in car for first time with Bwana, I fright.' She laughed at herself. The man laughed too and squeezed Ayah's shoulders tightly. His teeth were yellow like a rat's, and his shirt was dirty around the collar. Ayah began to feel uneasy, but he had been so kind, so like Bwana.

Down endless identical, carpeted corridors they lurched until the man produced a key and unlocked a door.

'My son is here?'

The man laughed. Ayah suddenly felt it was not a pleasant sound but the door shut behind her. She retreated until the dressing table dug into her thighs. Then, realising why he had brought her there, another possibility crossed her mind. A baby, a milk white baby could be hers, she imagined.

Ayah's dark daughter lay on a goatskin in her foster-mother's hut. Mumbi felt she had done her duty. She had offered the child her breast and the child had turned away. Mumbi sat in the village square and ground maize with the other women. When she had finished she plaited her hair and dreamed, not of her pompous husband but of her slim young lover.

Simeon's baby had ceased to be demanding. She had ceased to be fat and shiny like her father. No one took much notice of her any more except her old stepmother Wambui. When the day's weeding and wood gathering were done she would flick away the sleepy flies and bathe the crusted eyelids. She would hold the wasted baby against her shrivelled breasts and sing to her softly.

♦

Ayah lay naked and listened to the snoring. She felt bruised and crushed and cheated. She had been subjected to an act of brutality not love. Bwana would not have been like that, but a child might still be hers.

Ayah ran into the bathroom and vomited gin and bitter lemon into the toilet. She sat on the edge of the bath, wanting to go away but wondering if it would be bad manners to leave without saying goodbye. She was sticky all over but did not dare wash at the gleaming washbasin. She decided she could not wait for ever for the bwana to wake up so she got dressed, hunted under his heap of clothes for the key and let herself out.

Downstairs she saw Memsahib, leaning on the counter arguing with the receptionist.

'You find my son,' she demanded. 'I left him in the care of one of your ayahs.'

The receptionist rang for the hotel manager. Ayah flattened herself against the wall behind the postcards, hoping to be invisible. Memsahib saw Ayah and raised her eyebrows. Ayah shook her head and held out her hands to show their emptiness. She no longer felt the need to throw herself at Memsahib's feet. She now carried a white man's seed and was Memsahib's equal.

Ayah selected a postcard. Like a bird, her eye was caught by the brilliant yellow of the allamandas framing a view of the university. Ayah paid at the desk and walked self-consciously away. The doorkeeper bowed as she passed through the doors.

'You find your son?' he called after her down the steps, and sniggered. He knew what they came for, these black tarts.

Ayah hobbled to the bus stop. She bought a corn cob and nibbled hungrily at the charcoal-blackened kernels.

'You come drink?'

Ayah shook her head at the man and wiped her fingers on her hanky.

'You come dance?'

Ayah hoped the bus would come soon. She took the postcard from her bag. She had never seen the university but she might send the card to Isaac. That way Memsahib would be sure to read it too. On the other hand she imagined Simeon, Charity and Shamba reading and re-reading it over a pot of tea and envying her the grand city life. Perhaps she would send it to Simeon instead.

Ursula paced around the garden and wondered what Ayah had been doing in the hotel. Had she taken Isaac? It was unlikely but to be sure she had hurried to the door and watched Ayah walk alone down the street. Ayah's behaviour had been suspicious but Ursula did not believe her capable of such duplicity.

She wandered to the pool and watched the white children playing in the water. Isaac would like flippers she thought. She would buy him some tomorrow.

Back at the bird cage, Ursula remembered the humiliation of the morning. At that moment, she heard the shrill sound of children's voices coming from somewhere behind the building. Loudest among them she recognised Isaac's excited patter.

Through a squalid passageway, past the dustbins, Ursula found her son. He squatted barefoot in the dust surrounded by a little circle of enrapt black faces. His clothes were filthy. Like the child Jesus found in the Temple, he held forth in – pidgin English.

'Come with me,' said Ursula quietly.

Isaac stared at her without moving. He was enjoying himself. He had found some friends. He did not want to go back to the lonely room with only his mother for company. There was a silence in which Ursula stooped and picked up Isaac's leather shoes and turned to go. If only he would keep his shoes on.

'Come and I'll get you an ice cream,' called Ursula over her shoulder. Isaac stood up and followed and the laughter of children and servants followed him.

Ursula ran a hot bath and scrubbed Isaac hard.

'Where's my ice cream? I want my ice cream,' he yelled.

Ursula dropped his clothes into the rubbish bin and dragged him from the bath still shouting and crying.

'You promised, Mummy. You promised!' He went on and on until Ursula slapped him. Isaac bit her hard on the arm. Ursula slapped him again and they both wept with pain and frustration.

Ursula took a large white towel warm from the rail and wrapped it around Isaac. She held him close and he put his arms around her sobbing quietly.

'We will go home tomorrow,' she said. Home to the country air and space that were so important for a growing boy.

At Memsahib Stephanie's house, Ayah tried to tell her friend about her day, the hotel, the funeral, the beautiful white lady who haunted her.

'That Mary and baby Jesus,' said her friend. She pulled a shiny tin medallion on a chain from the front of her dress.

'See,' she said.

'Oooh.' Ayah looked at the tiny engraving of mother and child. As she touched the medal, sunlight reflected off it onto the walls of her friend's room. She sipped her tea and wished that she too could carry it around with her.

'You come Catholic, they give you one.'

Ayah knew she would go through fire and brimstone for such a treasure. She helped her friend prepare tea for the children. She bathed them and tucked them up in bed. She read them stories and sang and danced and the children were happy. Stephanie looked in, surprised by so much laughter.

'Why, Ayah,' she said, 'I didn't know you were here.' Ayah with her eyes on Memsahib's growing stomach could say nothing.

'I saw you at the funeral,' laughed Stephanie, 'in that wonderful dress.'

In the country, Simeon dreamt of mornings when the house sang with cooking bacon; when the dough rose high above the bowl's edge and the egg whisk chinked on china to make stiffly whipped cream to be piped into rich rosettes. His culinary skills were now wasted, he felt, on salads and baked beans on toast. His pay remained the same and the work was less, but the result was not satisfactory.

Ursula was amazed at the number of large brown envelopes that arrived in the post. At first she opened them and read the contents and signed and returned them as instructed. But there were so many of them. They couldn't all be necessary. And anyway, she had no intention of selling the farm.

'Why me?' she asked her lawyer. 'Why did they pick on me?'

'It's not just you. It's happening everywhere.'

'How will I live?'

'You will receive compensation in the UK.'

'But I am staying here,' insisted Ursula. She walked with Isaac under the jacarandas, hand in hand in the cool of the evening. She pushed the envelopes to the back of her mind and thought that all this was hers and nobody could take it away.

For two weeks Ayah lived in hope. Then she felt a wetness between her legs that she refused to believe. She put off going to the toilet until her bladder ached, then as she squatted in the latrines she had to accept the evidence of the red stain in her pants.

Ayah sat on the grass watching the children play while her friend pegged out the washing. Stephanie slept on the verandah in her swimsuit. Ayah wondered why the womb of Memsahib Stephanie should be so receptive while she, Ayah, bled.

Ayah crept closer and closer to the verandah. She thought she saw the flutter of tiny limbs pucker the flimsy material. Ayah stretched out her hand to touch and then the memsahib awoke, startled to see Ayah so near.

'You want I bring cup tea?' asked Ayah.

'She can't stay here for ever,' was Stephen's reaction.

'She can't stay here for ever,' Stephanie said to her ayah.

Through a friend Ayah heard of a family that required domestic help. The pay was only half the amount she had been getting, but it was a roof over her head and enough to live on.

'You come in, dear. Have a cup of tea,' shouted Mrs Mbaka

as a child opened the door. Frying fat filled the house with a warm, comfortable smell.

Ayah sat on the plastic settee amongst the bare-bottomed children. She was shocked by the chaos. A little boy crept up behind her and pushed her headscarf over her eyes. He ran off laughing while his mother shouted after him that he was a bad boy.

It was nice to feel one of the family though, thought Ayah, and waded into the mess with enthusiasm. She scraped up grime with a knife. She took the carpets outside to scrub on the patch of dusty lawn. She washed and mopped and dusted and cooked until she was exhausted.

'Please, you buy pants,' she asked her employer. They always spoke in English. Ayah felt the children's scruffiness reflected on her. She took some old curtains of Memsahib's from her trunk to make up dresses for the girls. She found an assortment of shoes and socks around the house which more or less fitted. She felt proud of the result when she lined up her little family.

Mrs Mbaka returned, immaculate from the city, and did not seem to notice. When the children came in for tea, dirty, torn and dusty she only said, 'What do you expect? Why you waste your time?' and Ayah began to wonder if it wouldn't be better not to bother.

'Memsahib,' Simeon said one day, gazing dolefully at his clean apron, 'Memsahib please, you find me new job.' A clean apron these days lasted him a week.

Ursula paused as she scooped out Isaac's boiled egg. Five servants for two people did seem a ridiculous expense. It would be sensible to get rid of Simeon.

'I will see what I can do,' she promised.

Isaac ran to fetch a book for his bedtime story. He drew up a stool so that he could see the pictures while Ursula read.

'What is that?' asked Isaac.

'A radiator. Hot water runs through the pipes and makes it warm. Look, through that window. There is snow outside.'

'Why does he have a radiator?'

'So he will not be cold.'

'Why will he be cold?'

'Because it is winter and the ground is covered in snow. In my country there is sometimes snow everywhere, like the white snow on top of the mountain.'

'I would like to see snow.'

'You can pick it up and shape it into balls. You can even make people out of it. Look here, on the next page, snowmen.'

'I would like to do that.'

'Perhaps you will one day.'

'Will you take me to your country, Mummy?'

Ursula laughed.

'Please, Mummy!'

'One day,' she said.

Ursula wrote to Stephanie about Simeon. She also wondered why she bothered to employ two shamba boys. Three gardeners to grow vegetables for one adult and one child who, in any case, lived on baked beans.

The end of the month came and went and Ayah had not received her pay. She slaved on, certain that Mrs Mbaka would remember and be overcome with remorse. One day she returned to her room to find her china shepherdess in fragments on the floor of her room. Another day a necklace was missing. They were items of no value except to Ayah, the carefully restored gleanings of Ursula's waste-paper basket.

Ayah bought a new padlock for the door and nailed cardboard over the broken window but the pilfering continued. She suspected the children and tried to catch them out. She was driven to tell her problems to Mrs Mbaka. Mrs Mbaka was affronted. She yelled and screamed and called Ayah a lazy slut and a liar.

Ayah, still unpaid, tried hiding her belongings – under the mattress, inside cushion covers, behind her chest. One by one her hidey-holes were discovered. Then her radio went. The shamba sat drunkenly on his doorstep and watched the weeds grow. The sound of music came from inside his room.

'You have new radio?'

'Yes, I have new radio.' He stood up and walked towards Ayah, a bottle in one hand, huge and threatening.

Ayah ran into her room and bolted the door. She wept with fear and exhaustion and yearned for the space and peace of Susan's home; for the smell of a hot iron gliding over white, laundered sheets; for birdsong as she gathered washing from the line; for the friendship and gossip of the other servants when the day's work was done.

Ayah decided she would visit her friend. She dried her hands when her day's work was done and approached her employer.

'Please you pay me money. I have visit my friend.'

Mrs Mbaka was painting her nails. Her hair, newly straightened and set, stuck out around her head like some monstrous beehive of steel wool.

'You get on Monday.'

'Please, I need money for bus.'

Mrs Mbaka sighed and opened her handbag which she kept always beside her. Ayah saw the purse bulging with notes and felt hopeful. Mrs Mbaka turned her back and extracted fifty cents. Ayah did not move.

'Please, I need one shillingi.'

'Well, you have walk one way,' snapped Mrs Mbaka and threw the coin on the carpet.

So Ayah walked from the native housing estate across the deserted Sunday city where pavements, saturated with heat, sent up a red-hot glare. Ayah stepped into the coolness of the red brick cathedral for a rest. The statue was still there, as beautiful as she remembered it. Ayah decided to use her fifty cents for a candle, just to see the figures come to life. It would be worth the walk home. The woman and child responded by dancing in the flickering light and Ayah's heart danced with them.

'How is baby today?' Ayah asked Memsahib Stephanie. She

looked bad-tempered and tired. The memsahib did not smile. Her sparkle was quenched.

'Baby is well, Memsahib?' asked Ayah, anxious now.

'Oh, baby is well.' Stephanie's legs ached after a morning of caring for the children. Her ayah had asked for the day off.

'I help you, Memsahib,' said Ayah and brought a footstool for her feet. In the fresh air and sunshine Ayah played cricket with the white children and wondered how she could face going back even for the sake of the money owed to her.

Stephanie arranged a lift home for Ayah in return for services rendered. Ayah found the children alone and hungry and wondered who would care for them after she had gone. She put bread and marge and a jug of water on the table.

'You wait,' she told the children, 'until your parents she come.'

When they arrived, Mrs Mbaka ate a slice of dry bread without sitting down. She had a white cardigan draped over her shoulders. She teetered over them in her white shoes with stiletto heels and pointed toes.

'Is this all?' she inquired, her voice sharp.

'Yes Madam, there is no more maize.'

'What you mean is no more maize? I buy maize last week.'

'Yes Madam, but the children have eat for lunch.'

'Is not good. They become fatty fatty.' She indicated with her hands the size one of her skinny children might attain in some far-off land of milk and honey.

Ayah left the house as soon as possible. She was grateful that the shamba sat on his doorstep in his customary drunken stupor. She feared that in some moment of sobriety he might rape her. She bolted the door and wedged a chair under the handle.

That evening she packed her bags. Memsahib's chauffeur had promised to collect her in the morning after he had taken Bwana to the office. She had no cash with which to repay such kindness but he was satisfied to take a pound of flesh instead.

CHAPTER 17

Ursula rang Stephen.

'What shall I do?' she asked.

'You haven't any choice. But if you sell now you'll get a better price than if you wait for a compulsory purchase order.'

'But what can I do? Where can I live?'

'Get a job and rent a house?'

'And Isaac?'

'You can always say he's a servant. He'll make a very good houseboy one day.'

So Ursula stopped opening the brown envelopes. She would put them on top of the pile on George's desk and then leave the room quickly shutting the door behind her. She wondered how a piece of paper could threaten her whole way of life and, more importantly, her relationship with Isaac. This was something beyond the range or understanding of officialdom, she decided, as the envelopes piled up unopened.

'Mummy,' called Isaac. 'Look at me!' Isaac could now clamber onto the lower branches of the jacarandas which suddenly looked fearfully high to Ursula. Her heart stood still as she ran to catch Isaac. Her chest was bruised by the small body that streaked down from the sky, but she caught him and laughed with relief.

'That was a good jump, Isaac.'

'Why did you get in the way, Mummy? You spoilt it.'

♦

Shamba spent much of his time polishing a car that was never used. He experimented with it cautiously, first backing it out of the garage, then driving round the front flowerbed. Then a little way up the drive. He grew maize over the greater part of the vegetable garden which he sold at the local market. To take the maize by car would save time and trouble, though the trouble was chiefly Charity's, since she carried the maize on her back. Still, if Shamba could transport more than one woman could carry, he could grow more. He imagined the orders flooding in.

Ayah sat in front of the still Memsahib in church and wondered what she thought, whether commercial exploitation of the body was perhaps not quite right? But what could be worse, she wondered, than scrubbing, cleaning and cooking for sixteen hours a day? Now she lived comfortably for a lot less effort. She earned enough for bus fares, food and rent and still had time to visit Memsahib Stephanie and this silent white memsahib and child that she had come to feel were her family.

At the suggestion of Stephanie's chauffeur and with his help, Ayah moved downtown. She arrived at the eastern edge of the concrete city and saw the whole of Mathare Valley before her, a desolate sprawl of shacks made of every material imaginable, except bricks or concrete. From time to time the city council bulldozers moved in and flattened this sore on the outskirts of the town but like a pruned plant it grew more vigorously than before.

The house Ayah lived in teetered on the brink in pink-stuccoed splendour, separated from the misery below by a slope too steep to allow anything to be built on its shifting surface.

The garden was a drinking parlour where bottled beer was sold under licence but most of the trade was in liquor brewed from the trickle of water that threaded its way through the sludge of the valley. Some thirty people lived in the five rooms of the house, but Ayah was fortunate. The chauffeur had influence and obtained the single room necessary for her trade.

'Now I live in a house like Memsahib,' Ayah said to herself as she bolted the door behind her and marvelled that anyone should think of paying her for anything so easy.

She had learned a lot about the white woman's way of life. Her room was tribute to this knowledge, a masterpiece of architectural improvisation. A house had to have many rooms. This Ayah achieved with strings and curtains. There was a kitchen with a paraffin stove dangerously close to the surrounding draperies. There was a dining room with table and chairs made from packing cases draped with gaudy cotton runners crotcheted in her spare time. Here there was a selection of Memsahib's cutlery, some glued crockery and an egg whisk that jammed on every turn. The largest area was the sitting room which contained an armchair with broken springs placed carefully over a thin rug to cover the holes. That too was a gift from Memsahib. Ayah pinned magazine pictures and a selection of old Christmas cards on the curtain walls.

She lavished most attention, however, on the bedroom where she plied her trade. In a glass vase on the sill of the only window, were her plastic flowers. Here hung the only electric light. Ayah arranged a rectangle of white crotchet over the red plastic shade and was pleased by the pink glow that speckled the walls and bed.

Memsahib had not considered electricity suitable or necessary for the servants. Bulbs were so often broken. By Ayah's time all that remained in the servants' quarters were shredded cords dangling from the roof timbers and a broken switch inside each door – which proved Memsahib right.

'Why should they need light anyway?' she asked, since everyone knew that natives lived by the sun.

Ayah poured water from an enamelled jug into her saucepan and made posho. Already potential clients were knocking on the door, but Ayah was tired. There was plenty of time tomorrow. Today she wanted to sit back and enjoy her home and her dream of the job she would one day find where there would be a white baby to love and care for.

♦

Her friend, Stephanie's ayah, had queued in the sun for three hours after the Memsahib heard a rumour that a certain shop had milk to sell. She returned empty-handed and weary to meet Memsahib asking her to work on her day off.

Stephanie too was tired and cross. Her garden was a wasteland where dust drifted like snow.

'But I need you to work on Sundays,' she wailed. 'Just look at me! How can I manage?'

'I ask Ayah. She come.'

Both ayahs were delighted. Sundays became the highlight of Ayah's week. The tight-waisted dresses of Ursula's youth were set aside in favour of plain white cotton, an apron and hat. Ayah walked as far as the cathedral where she stopped to light a candle and then continued on her way by matatu. Her friend left more and more work for her to do and Ayah enjoyed every minute of her day. On Mondays she returned to her trade and counted the days as they went by, drawing on her small reservoir of happiness.

On those weekdays, Ayah catered for the needs of the lonely and displaced – the cooks, gardeners and chauffeurs – far away from their villages and families. She gave each a taste of warmth and understanding. For a brief period they felt like human beings.

Ursula watched over Isaac, anxious that he should be always happy, ready to forestall the first sign of anxiety or displeasure. She helped build fantastic towers out of bricks supporting them so that they would not topple over. She ordered boxes of toys to keep him amused. His clothes were impeccable. His skin had acquired a glow and his eyes shone, her womb contracted when he called her 'Mummy'.

In her long, loose caftans, Ursula hovered over the child. She could please herself what she wore and when she ate. The needs of farm and animals which governed her husband's day no longer applied. Once a week the farm manager called with groceries and a money order. Sometimes Ursula saw him herself, but she preferred to send Charity's daughter to the door.

Books arrived from London in heavy cartons with such titles

as *How to Educate Your Child at Home* or *A Child's Early Needs* and Ursula devoured them all. She sellotaped charts along the walls of the corridor between the toilet and the nursery. They related to the various developmental stages of childhood which she could not in turn relate to her living child. But then, she reflected, her circumstances were unique. There was no cause for concern.

'What does she think I am, an employment agency?' Stephanie asked her husband. She thought of Simeon's mouth-watering recipes, the soufflés and extravaganzas of cream and avocado.

'The man is worth his weight in gold,' she said and they both giggled at the preposterous thought.

'I already have a cook,' she replied, 'but town is the best place to be if he wants a job. Why doesn't he come and stay with his wife?' Stephanie smiled and wondered what would happen when Simeon saw what his wife was up to. She shifted uncomfortably in her chair. She suffered much pain, as if the baby's head rested on a nerve.

Ursula laid aside her sewing and watched Isaac. He lay back in his chair on the verandah, his small face turned up towards the cloudless sky. Like a pansy, she thought, deep and velvet and soft. The post this morning, flung on top of the mountain on George's desk, had caused a landslide. Soon the envelopes would overflow into the corridor.

Charity wandered from room to room, idly flicking a duster. There was little washing up to do and only Memsahib's washing since Memsahib insisted on doing Isaac's laundry herself.

Ursula wondered why her hands had become so chapped. The nails were brittle though she filed and polished them and applied handcream after each immersion in soapy water.

Nor did Charity's hands improve with their new leisure. They had become unaccustomed to the hoe and the panga and her palms were blistered and bloodied. Shamba insisted on help in the vegetable garden and allowed no respite.

It was so hot that Ursula sat dreaming of the sea.

'Let us go on holiday, Isaac.'

'On holiday?'

'Yes. To the sea.'

'What about my present?'

It was nearly Christmas. Memsahib had promised Isaac a bike, like the one that went to the orphanage and nearly broke Isaac's heart. A red shiny bike with handlebars of silver.

'We could take your present with us.'

'How big is it?' Isaac's soul was filled with suspicion.

'You will love the sea,' she said. 'It is so big and tastes of salt. At the edges are beaches made of sand.' Ursula imagined herself on the beach with Isaac, the sand like icing sugar between her toes. She wandered in a gentle breeze under the coconut palms and held coral and sea shells glistening in her hand. Isaac was a dark silhouette against the sparkling waves. Just the two of them.

Isaac dreamed of other children who clamoured after him wanting a go on his red bike. White children begging and pleading, and he would say no. He wandered down the garden to find Shamba.

'Shamba, have you seen the sea?'

Shamba shook his head. He wished he could impress his son.

'Look,' he said. He squatted down and showed the child a dung beetle pushing along the ground a ball of dung many times larger than itself. Laboriously it progressed towards its hole with what would become the nursery for a whole new generation. At the top of the mound it paused and raised its shovel head as the ball plopped into the hole. At that moment Shamba jabbed a twig into the centre of its back beneath the wing casing. The beetle uttered a low deep buzz and became a tangled mass of legs.

'Is for you,' said Shamba, handing the stick to his son.

'Memsahib, Simeon is here. He want see you.'

'Not now. Tell him I'm resting,' said Stephanie. Her baby had grown so large that even the thought of food was painful.

She suffered from heartburn and a permanently bitter taste in her mouth.

'Why do they all come to me? All Ursula's wretched servants. Why can't she look after them herself?'

Simeon went to Ayah's house.

'You bad woman,' he said and beat her.

'What else can I do?' she wailed. He would find out for himself what it was like, traipsing from door to door with his crumpled references. His hat would sag in the heat and dust like a mousse too long out of the refrigerator.

Isaac carried the beetle triumphantly home, a soldier with his banner, goose-stepping with back straight, knees lifted high at each step, blowing a trumpet noise through closed, vibrating lips. He marched up the verandah steps and dropped the offering onto Ursula's lap.

'For you, Mummy,' and he saluted.

Ursula screamed and swept everything off her knee. She jumped to her feet in tears of shock and outrage.

'How could you?' she shrieked. 'Get off the verandah.'

Ursula bent to retrieve her reels of cotton, the pin tin, needle case and skeins of silk. Underneath, she found the beetle, shaken free of the stick, it lay on its back with its legs pawing in slow motion at the air.

Ursula held up her long skirt and stamped hard. There was a crunch and then Isaac started screaming.

'You killed my beetle! You killed my beetle!'

'Go away and play,' said Ursula. She hopped towards the lawn to wipe her shoe clean.

'But you told me not to kill things.' Isaac knelt on the concrete and stared at the green and black slime that had been his beetle.

'You are a bad mummy.'

The grass rains came and Stephanie watched with sadness as the last blossom was battered off the jacarandas and washed in lilac streams along the gutter. The reservoirs would fill and she could have her shower.

Ayah arrived with her legs and clothes splattered with mud. Downtown was awash with rivers of mud and even at the end of Memsahib Stephanie's road, she had had to wade through a turgid river before reaching the higher ground of the avenue.

The memsahib was approaching the date of her confinement and Ayah looked at her anxiously. The memsahib was so thin. Her own memsahib had become enormous before Susan's birth, like some monstrous ball on stilts. Ayah feared for this baby. The Memsahib should eat more and fatten her child.

'Memsahib, you think baby is boy or girl?'

'I don't know.'

'What you want, Memsahib?'

'I don't mind.'

'I have friend, Memsahib, she come tell you if it is boy or girl.'

'I'll wait and see, thank you.'

'It very easy, Memsahib. She put hand on stomach, like this, and she tell you.'

'Take your hands off me!'

Ayah recoiled, but she had felt the hard lump of the baby's heel pressing against the taut skin, and felt reassured.

Simeon set off on his door-to-door rounds. He carried his recipe books pungent with the smell of newly baked bread, crusty and adorned with sesame seeds. Who would be able to resist his sponges which rose to unprecedented heights?

His heart was high with hope. He had money in his pocket, which Ayah had given him before she locked him out of her room for the day. He checked to see that his references were safe in the breast pocket of one of Bwana's old jackets. The sleeves were short and tight, for Bwana had been a long lean man, but it was a suit. The shirt-collar pinched and soon his bare ankles were rubbed raw, but at the bus stop people stood aside to let him pass. Crowds parted before him.

But the dogs at the gates of the white men's houses snarled and bared their teeth. Simeon looked at them and laughed. They were only animals!

♦

In the country Shamba's maize grew and so did the grass. Then the mower broke down and Shamba did not know how to repair it. The farm manager promised to look at it one day but he was a busy man with important things on his mind. Even Memsahib did not suggest using a panga, she too had come to rely on the machine.

A jungle sprung up around the house. Water poured over the edge of blocked gutters breaking plants and sweeping away the topsoil in dark sludgy channels.

Ursula realised that there had been no more brown envelopes for a long time. It was then that the phone started to ring. It seemed to Ursula as though it rang all the time. When it was silent she tiptoed past, fearful of jolting it into life. She tried leaving the receiver off but then a high-pitched whine followed her wherever she went.

Charity was kept too busy in the fields by Shamba to do any housework, so she sent for her daughter. Her daughter came, poorly sighted, hard of hearing and pathetically grateful to be wanted. She hoed for Shamba and she cleaned for Memsahib and the stock of crockery in the china pantry diminished day by day. At night she took her turn sleeping with Shamba.

Shamba reflected that in the dark Charity's daughter was all right. She was young and warm and he tried to forget how much she irritated him during the day with her clumsy forays into his garden.

Shamba's money jingled in his pocket as he stomped around his vegetable plot watching the women at work. He was saving up for a radio. After that perhaps for a wife. A proper wife this time, not one he could lose like Ayah. Charity and her daughter were not quite the same as wives, but they could remain for as long as they were useful.

Ursula and Isaac sat on the verandah with plates balanced on their knees and the washing tickling the back of Ursula's neck. Ursula had hung a piece of string along the verandah which saved walking through the long grass down the garden to the washing line. She positioned the chairs carefully to avoid drips and congratulated herself that drying in the shade would preserve the colours of the garments.

Books continued to arrive though Ursula could not remember having ordered them all. She looked in dismay at the yawning gulf between what she ought to be doing, and what was possible. She gave up reading and stacked the books along the corridor. Isaac used them as seats or flicked over the pages looking for pictures. His thumbs were so black on the paper, alien beings in a world of playgroups and tea parties and outings to the park.

His life was now calm and predictable. There was little by way of surprise or laughter. He pottered quietly after his mother through their shrinking world.

In the airless pantry, Ursula scratched her arms where the mosquitoes bit and made up her shopping order for the week. Their diet now consisted almost entirely of tins, vegetables and meat, processed and bland, and slices of flabby white bread. Even the eggs from the local store were not fresh.

So Ursula with the help of Charity's daughter moved the hen house to the lawn below the verandah to be sure of having fresh eggs. Ursula was certain that the servants ate them so now, when a hen went broody, she shut her in a coop on a clutch of eggs.

'Look Isaac,' she said, 'baby chicks will come out of those eggs, all golden like the sun.'

Isaac poked a twig into the dingy cage and the hen snapped viciously with its head tilted to one side.

'You mustn't do that, Isaac. You must not hurt things.'

In the mornings when Ursula and Isaac got up, they would sometimes find gifts laid on the verandah steps; avocados or limes, mangos shaped like tear drops, or passion fruit from the creeper over the septic tank.

One morning Ursula and Isaac held warm eggs up to their ears and heard a faint cheep and tapping inside.

'Soon Isaac, they will break the shell and come out.'

The last gas cylinder for the cooker ran out. Shamba offered to sell Memsahib charcoal, made from her own trees, as she pointed out.

'But I make the charcoal,' he said. He sold Ursula some maize cobs as well and Charity's daughter demonstrated how to set up a barbecue on the verandah.

'What fun this is,' said Ursula, while Isaac laughed and crunched crisp blackened corn kernels and the greasy smoke stained the washing. When Ursula found her saucepans burnt on the bottom Charity swopped them for some cheap ones from the local market.

Each day passed in a crescendo and diminuendo of heat and light. Ursula tied back her long hair in a pony tail to keep it out of the way. Isaac brought vanilla frangipani to thread through the ribbon so that Ursula moved in a halo of fragrance.

The chicks hatched. They found them in the coop one morning, eight fluffy golden tennis balls.

'How soft they are, Mummy,' said Isaac. He held one in the palm of his hand. It was as light as thistledown. He rubbed it against his cheek like a golden powder puff and a smile spread over his face.

Later Ursula found one of the chicks gasping in the dust with its entrails hanging out. She hadn't seen what had happened but assumed that Charity's daughter had trodden on it. Ursula fetched a big stick and closed her eyes as she hit the tiny creature over and over again. She could not bear to see it suffer.

Simeon wandered from house to house. He accepted Ayah's food and shelter but refused her money. On his long walks to the white areas of the city he tied his shoelaces together and draped the shoes round his neck. He was afraid they would become shabby with the miles he covered. Though he never spoke to them he began to recognise other figures plodding the same weary course. Without realising it, he developed the same hopeless, nasal whine as he leaned over gates waving his references.

Ayah visited the clinic for her three-monthly injection and

wondered whether to tell them how much she was bleeding. She decided it was a small price to pay to be rid of the fear of pregnancy and said nothing. Then she went into town and bought herself a new dress, white with enormous scarlet poppies. In a moment of rashness she also bought shoes and a bag in white patent plastic. She had never bought anything new before and was frightened at her own extravagance. She justified it as being necessary for her work, since it was important that she always looked her best.

Charity's daughter showed Memsahib how to scour her saucepans with sand. Ursula rubbed the harsh grains into the sticky lumps of scrambled egg with her fingers, then swilled water round and round until the tin gleamed. She wondered at the quantity of detergent she had once bought.

Then one day the mother hen vanished. Ursula stared in disbelief at the narrow bars and wondered how it could possibly have got out. She hoped the chicks were large enough to survive on their own.

'Where did you get that feather from?' she asked Isaac sharply. Isaac sat cross-legged on the floor stroking his arm with a feather corrugated and striped like black and white knitting.

'Shamba gave it to me.'

Ursula knew it was from her hen yet she feared making a scene. The fact that Shamba was Isaac's natural father was always at the back of her mind these days. He strutted round like the cock of the farmyard. She could almost hear him crow and was afraid.

Ursula locked and bolted the front door and hid the key. She did the same with the back door leading to the servants' quarters so that Charity's clumsy daughter could only enter through the verandah. All the windows were closed and the air became stale and hot inside the house making a haven for mosquitoes.

Ursula insisted that Isaac always kept within sight. If he was in the house she sat on the verandah like a guard. If he went down the garden she followed like a shadow.

Charity's daughter lit a fire night and morning so that Isaac could bathe. Twice a day Ursula scrubbed him and put him in clean clothes. Charity's daughter kindled the fire with books from the stacks in the corridor though she kept the pictures that appealed to her. She wondered if it was good for a child, the way Memsahib scrubbed him so often.

Ursula jumped if a twig snapped or a cup broke in the kitchen. When her manager brought the post or groceries and she heard his car on the gravel drive she hid in the bedroom with her hand over Isaac's mouth. Isaac no longer jumped and sang and laughed. He had become quiet and serious like his mother. He clung to her skirts, wide-eyed and fearful, and if he could not find her, he panicked, screaming with some irrational fear.

Isaac was learning to count.

'One two five, nine, ten, eleven,' he chanted triumphantly as he played. Ursula began again, patiently numbering the fingers of her right hand.

'Look, Isaac:

> One, two, three four five,
> Once I caught a fish alive . . .'

They counted the chicks each morning when they opened the coop.

'One, two, three, four, five, six, seven, eight,' Isaac recited without fault, his eyes following the track of a large bumble bee. It buzzed from flower to flower, its wings a silver blur in the sunlight. Then the bee landed on a flower and waggled its bottom like a spring lamb who has found its mother's teat.

'No. There are only seven, Isaac.'

A couple of days later, there were only six.

'Where do they go?' Ursula asked Charity's daughter.

'Snake, she eat.' The lumpish girl squinted around and prodded at the undergrowth with her toes.

'Here is too much leaves. Is not good, Memsahib.'

'Shamba should deal with this,' said Ursula, squatting over the charcoal and fanning the flames with the telephone directory.

Charity's daughter nodded. Memsahib was quite right.

'You tell Shamba to come.' Ursula would not tell him herself. She avoided direct contact with him at all costs, just as she shunned the brown envelopes and visitors and anything that posed a threat to her life with Isaac. She had seen Shamba's eyes follow the child. She knew where the chicks had gone, although once the snake had been suggested she began to imagine the flick of a dark tail each time she went onto the verandah.

Every night as she lay next to Shamba, Charity's daughter tried to give voice to Memsahib's order to cut back the shrubs and grass around the verandah. It was such a simple request but the words never got as far as her lips. They went round and round in her mind until she really thought she had asked him.

Ursula remembered reading somewhere that snakes dislike the smell of geraniums. Armed with secateurs, and with Isaac trotting by her side, Ursula foraged among the ruins of the garden. Somewhere she knew, there had once been geraniums. Eventually she found them, gawky, straggling things battling through the undergrowth towards light and warmth.

With help from Charity's daughter, Ursula and Isaac cleared a narrow strip of soil in front of the verandah. Ursula made holes in the soil with a kitchen spoon. She did not like to ask Shamba where the gardening tools were kept and they were no longer in the shed.

Isaac carried pots of water splish, splash from the bathroom across the abandoned sitting room. He poured them carefully around the geranium cuttings.

'Little pools, Mummy,' he cried with delight, dabbling his fingers in the mud.

'Don't do that, Isaac, you'll get dirty.' His mother feared the dirt that would be invisible on his dark skin.

Ursula's dress clung to her back and thighs. Sweat poured down her forehead and dripped off the tip of her nose before the job was done. She could have been any labourer's wife squatting in her garden, her face dark in the shade of her hunched shoulders, watched by her wide-eyed toto.

At last the fragile line of defence was completed, a spindly row of sticks that might take root. Ursula felt better when the job was done. Isaac was responsible for watering the plants night and morning but even so the heart-shaped leaves wilted and fell. Ursula began to wonder whether any would survive.

'We will give them one more week,' she said. Then one morning there was a tiny green shoot. It sprouted from the side of a stalk given up for dead. Then another. The plants were alive and Ursula felt safe.

The number of chicks remained constant at four, and another hen was broody. Ursula moved the chicks into an old wooden beer crate, covered with an upturned coffee table, to vacate the coop for the broody hen. Two chicks vanished on the first night and Ursula realised too late that she had forgotten to block off the hand holes.

In an empty garage, Charity now hand-reared five chickens. Their legs were growing longer. They lost their baby appeal and dark shades of flight feathers, barred black and white, appeared on their tiny wings. Charity dreamed of her stall at market, next to the patch where Shamba sold his maize. Her heap of fat squawking hens would be the best on sale, and the pyramid of speckled eggs the talk of the town.

Ursula shut the chicks in the living room at night where there was nothing more threatening than mosquitoes and tiny transparent geckos who moved silently on suckered feet over the curtains and ceiling.

But one day they escaped. Someone left the door open, and though Ursula briefly wondered who was to blame, she decided it didn't much matter. The damage was done and by that nightfall only one chick came home to roost.

CHAPTER 18

It was mid-morning by the time Charity's daughter brought tea, one cup and one mug poured from the lukewarm dregs of the pot Charity and Shamba had been drinking. There was no longer a tray with embroidered cloth or tiny slices of toast wrapped in a napkin, only the cups to add to the rings on the bedside cupboard.

Nor was there any need to draw back the curtains. They had not been drawn in the weeks since George's funeral. Hot rain and heavy sun had goaded the golden shower to a rate of growth that could almost be measured day by day. Now it hung in a thick pall over the window.

'Tea's here, Isaac,' said Ursula. A small black arm crept up from beneath the bedclothes and twined round her neck.

'Did you have a nice sleep?' he mumbled.

Ursula plumped up the pillows and they sat side by side sipping their drinks. In the freckled light that filtered through greenery stirred by gentle currents of air, shadows darkened Ursula's skin. Columns of dust danced in narrow rays of sunshine. It was a green underwater world where darkness and light rippled in unending motion.

Ursula put down her empty cup and glided towards the dressing table. Isaac watched as she combed her long dark hair. Was there anyone as beautiful as his mummy in the whole world, he wondered.

'Mummy,' he said. 'It's too dark in here. We'd better tell Shamba to cut down some of those branches.'

'Why, Isaac? I like it like this.'

'But, Mummy, I can't see out.'

Ursula thought of the houses that Isaac drew on the backs of all those brown envelopes. The painting paper was long since used up. She thought his pictures were wonderful, as if no child before had ever drawn such people and animals and cars. But, his houses!

'You've left out the windows again,' she was at last driven to comment.

'But it's like our house, Mummy. You can't see the windows because of the bushes. They have a lazy shamba!'

Ursula, still brushing her hair could hear the telephone ringing. She wondered whether Charity's daughter would answer it, or not. It didn't really matter.

But Charity's daughter was sweeping out her mother's room and heard nothing above the rasping of the twig-broom on the concrete. Charity and Shamba, still sitting in the sun with a silver teapot between them, did hear.

'Perhaps if I run, I get there in time?' said Charity. More likely, by the time she had run across the yard, past the washing line, round the septic tank, up the verandah steps and into the living room it would have stopped.

Still Ursula brushed her hair.

'Telephone, Mummy,' said Isaac, watching the shadows.

'Let her answer it herself,' thought Charity. 'Why should I run?'

'I'll go,' said Shamba at last since no one else moved. Perhaps it was for him, the corn-cob magnate. Visions of orders flooded his mind, people clamouring for his maize. Beneath the coarse-grained, papery leaves the golden nuggets gleamed brighter than on any other stall in the market. He put on his shoes and ran. In the sitting room he reached out to pick up the receiver but the line was dead.

'Hello, hello!' he called and peered down the mouthpiece, shaking the instrument.

'Who is it?' called Ursula from the bedroom. 'Just say I am not here.'

Simeon returned to Ayah's room with the daily newspaper. He sat with his feet stuck straight out in front of him, his bulk filling the entire living area and his elbows jutting through the curtains into the kitchen. With a pencil, he carefully ringed any Situations Vacant that might be suitable.

Ayah bustled around with a duster and dustpan and brush to have the place tidy before the day's work began.

'Why you not cook breakfast?' she asked wearily. She lit the paraffin stove and put on a saucepan of water.

'I am cook, not African woman,' replied Simeon. He would not cook posho over paraffin. He had lost weight and now seemed shrunken inside huge loose rolls of spare flesh. He chewed with distaste at the hard white balls of meal that Ayah handed him. 'Why you not get job? We work together and be happy, like at Memsahib's.'

Ayah wondered if he would ever learn. She shrugged and handed over a pile of coins. Simeon had a new theory, that making an appointment by telephone was more impressive than calling at the gate like a beggar.

Ayah was happy. Today she would call at Memsahib Stephanie's before starting work. The memsahib was near her time and Ayah had decided to visit mid-week as well as on Sundays just to keep an eye on things. Today she would help her friend take the sweet-smelling clothes from the washing line. She would smooth them with a hot iron and sip tea and smell the dinner cooking.

Ayah put on her new dress, the one with the huge scarlet poppies, and her white plastic handbag and shoes.

Ursula took a bucket of water to swill down the verandah. The chickens made such a mess. She swilled and swept, brushing the mess before her while Isaac, who would have loved to help, watched from where she had sat him, on the table.

The operation also watered the geraniums below. The first of the cuttings was in bloom. The foliage was luxuriant, fertilised by chicken droppings. The leaves had fanned out to become deep-veined and fleshy. Ursula found their scent distasteful and assumed that her remedy would be all the more effective for being unpleasant.

She brought the last chick out of the box in the sitting room. Isaac sprinkled a handful of corn and it pecked at the floor with a small staccato noise. Like any young animal it needed company and soon made its way down the steps to join the hens from the hen house below the verandah in the soft dust and leafy shade. Ursula noticed sadly that its last patch of golden down was replaced by rather dull feathers.

Simeon was on his eighth phone call.

'Hello? I read paper, you need cook. I very good cook. You give me ad–dress, I come show you.'

The line went dead. Simeon shook the receiver. He thumped his fist on the coin box and wondered what was wrong. The same thing happened every time. It must be a faulty phone.

The phone rang in Ursula's house just as Charity's daughter was frying okra for lunch. She did not trust the telephone and held it out at arm's length. She said nothing.

'Hello. Hello! came the voice. 'Could I speak to the memsahib?' The request was repeated in Swahili but Charity's daughter did not speak that language either. Unhurriedly she lurched through the house and back onto the verandah. Shading her eyes, she blinked through the waist-high grass, through the gap between the top of the banisters and the cascasdes of purple bougainvillea drifting from the roof.

'Memsahib, phone . . .' she bellowed and fought her way through the greasy black smoke back to her frying pan. Half an hour later Ursula and Isaac appeared for lunch.

'Memsahib, I not find you. A man, she ring.'

Ursula picked up the phone but there was no one there.

Simeon decided to go home and spend his remaining money on beer. He walked slowly, not so much because of his size, but because a great depression weighed him down.

He sat at a table with his head in his hands and looked down into the valley. His beer arrived and his back straightened and he raised his eyes to higher hopes. This afternoon he would be lucky. Perseverance was necessary. If a memsahib would only allow him to cook one meal . . .

And there was Ayah coming out of the front door in her new outfit – a fit accoutrement for any gentleman, to sit at his table, so that all who saw would envy him. He stood up smiling and beckoning. Ayah, who had not noticed Simeon at all in her haste to be gone, was annoyed.

'You have beer?' invited her husband.

Ayah shook her head and sat down reluctantly.

'Why you not have beer?'

'I have lemonade,' she said. Every second was precious this afternoon but she did not want to spoil Simeon's good humour.

'This afternoon,' he said, 'I find work. I go Westlands, to big houses.' He smiled and indicated their size with his arms and dreamed of the good ingredients within.

Ayah smiled politely and knew it was the beer talking.

'I even find work for you, my wife!'

At Memsahib Stephanie's house, Ayah's friend polished the pram. It was a beautiful pram with gleaming chrome and a navy-blue padded body. Her friend arranged a blue and white gingham parasol to one side and showed Ayah how to adjust it to keep the sun off the baby's face.

'Look. You tip like this.'

Ayah tried. The apparatus danced on its spring and the white lace jiggled. Then it tumbled off the clip into the dust. The ayah laughed and shook it clean.

'He must be tightly, this hook.'

'Like this?' asked Ayah.

'Memsahib Stephanie, she go hospital last night.'

Ayah could not speak because of a sudden breathlessness.

'She had baby girl. Bwana, she very pleased.'

Ayah rubbed the hem of her new dress along the handle to remove fingermarks. She imagined the baby of Bwana George all golden and white, wrapped in soft white clothes, So delicate!

'She come home Saturday.'

'Oh,' said Ayah. For the day after Memsahib Stephanie's return was Sunday. *Her* day.

Ursula was in the middle of Isaac's bedtime story when the phone rang again.

'Don't stop now Mummy,' begged Isaac.

'I'll hurry back.' Ursula walked over to the telephone leaving a trail of footprints in the dust.

'Hello.'

'Ursula. Hello, how are you?'

'Stephen!'

'Yes. Stephanie asked me to ring you. She had a baby girl early this morning.'

'Is everything all right?'

'Yes. I tried to ring early this morning but nobody answered. Then at lunchtime someone answered but you never came. I waited a long time then gave up.'

'Oh. I was in the garden.'

'Naomi is especially pleased to have a sister. She would like to talk to you.'

'Not now, Stephen, I'm just putting Isaac to bed.'

Stephen rang off feeling guilty. How would he have felt, he wondered, if he had lost a daughter.

'A girl,' thought Ursula. George would have been pleased. She would remember to send flowers in the morning.

Before she went to bed, Ursula shut up the hens. The chick was not with them. She searched the nearby gardens on her hands and knees, parting the jungle of grass stalks and calling gently. She looked behind the sack of charcoal on the verandah and moved all the furniture. As dusk became darkness, her despair gave way to a curious sense of relief.

'Now the snake will leave us alone,' she thought. 'There is nothing more it can take from me.'

Ayah returned home in the evening to find Simeon already in bed. She did not need to ask how his day had gone. Ayah slid her tin trunk from under her bed and unlocked it.

'What you doing?' Simeon rolled laboriously onto his side to watch.

'Looking for clothes. Memsahib Stephanie, she have baby girl.' Ayah's eyes glowed. She unpacked tiny vests and nightdresses, small white cardigans with pearl buttons, crumpled dresses of broderie anglaise. She unfolded each garment slowly and smoothed it against her knee.

'Where you get those?'

'From Memsahib.'

'She give them?'

Ayah shook her head. The parcel should have gone to the orphanage but Bwana had given them to her, for her daughter who was too large and ugly to wear the delicate fabrics. Tomorrow, Ayah would take them to Susan's sister. Perhaps not all of them. Not at once. It gave her such pleasure to know that they were there in her room.

Tomorrow, thought Simeon, he would call on the memsahib, to offer his congratulations and ask for work. At such a time surely, the memsahib's beneficence would overflow.

Ayah wrapped one vest, one cardigan and one nightdress in a fine white shawl and put them in her shopping bag. Then she slept, as she had done since Simeon's arrival, perched precariously on the edge of the narrow bed clinging to her husband.

The next morning, she woke early. Ayah fetched a bucket of cold water from the bathroom upstairs and scrubbed herself from head to toe. Hygiene was important with young babies, Memsahib had taught her. Ayah even scrubbed her short curly hair. She put on her best uniform, carefully folded and smelling of mothballs. She wanted to look her best.

Ayah arrived at the memsahib's house while Memsahib Stephanie was sitting up in her hospital bed in a frilly pink bed jacket eating breakfast. She had paid more for her room (in advance) than she would for the most expensive hotel in town and the toast was like leather. She cupped her hands round her tea and looked through the windows at the sunlight on the trees and grass and the glowing beds of deep red cannas.

She felt cheated because she had chosen to share a room with three other women rather than be on her own even though it meant that her baby would have to remain in the nursery. She had looked forward to the company. But she had not been able to specify the colour of the other women and it had been a shock at first. Perhaps there was a mistake? she queried.

But the sister in charge arranged the women according to the number of children they had. Few white women had as many as four babies, they mostly had more sense.

'I shan't have any more,' Stephanie had announced.

'What you have?'

'Two boys and two girls.' She was rewarded with gasps of admiration and envy.

'I have six girls. I come every year until I have son,' said a woman who was knitting luminous orange baby clothes. The others clucked in sympathy.

Stephanie had been surprised by these bloated black lumps who gasped and groaned, rang for the nurse and begged for pain-killers in front of their husbands – if their husbands visited. Those who did come ignored their wives and read newspapers or chatted among themselves.

Surely, having a baby should come naturally to them, Stephanie thought. She slipped out of bed and stretched her arms above her head, so slim in her transparent nightdress.

'I'm off for a shower,' she said. She wanted to look her best when Stephen came to collect her.

At Stephanie's home, Ayah and her friend sat on the doorstep drinking tea and looked out for the car that would bring the memsahib and her baby home. Ayah's friend was short-tempered after looking after the children for the previous forty-eight hours.

'Mummy's coming home today, Mummy's coming home today,' sang Naomi, skipping and scuffing her toes through the gravel.

'You make shoes dirty,' snapped Ayah's friend.

'Then you can clean them again,' said Naomi. She stuck out her tongue and skipped away through the house door. Ayah was shocked.

♦

As Stephanie's chauffeur turned right out of the narrow hospital gateway, a flower van charged gaily in.

'You bloody well look where you're going,' shouted Stephen, fearful for his wife and child.

The driver laughed with a flash of white teeth, after all what was a skid and a squeal of brakes? He accelerated away showering Stephen in dust.

Ursula's flowers were delivered to the maternity wing, imported spring flowers in a vast, cellophane-wrapped bunch secured by a yellow paper ribbon. Pink would have been too corny, thought Ursula, and would have clashed with the daffodils.

The nurses didn't know what to do with the bouquet. They dumped the flowers in empty milk bottles on the table in the centre of the ward that Stephanie had left. The only other flowers were on her abandoned locker together with bowls of grapes and peaches that she hadn't bothered to take away. The lockers of the other ladies were bare.

When Stephanie's car pulled up, Ayah hurried forward. She opened the door and held out her arms. She saw the golden downy head and her heart melted.

'She just like Bwana.'

Stephanie looked up, tense and suddenly watchful. Only when she heard the voice did she realise that the pair of black arms belonged to Ayah.

'I'm flattered,' said Stephen and laughed. Stephanie smiled and relaxed.

'What are you doing here today?' she asked.

The next day was Sunday, Ayah's day. Stephanie sat on the verandah, pleased to be at home, and smoked a cigarette. She wore a tight-waisted skirt and felt as if the past nine months had never existed.

'You look wonderful,' said Stephen, so that even the arrival of Simeon did not distress Stephanie. He approached like a dusty black beetle and she realised it was in her power to crush him. But today was a happy day and tomorrow she would give a party so that everyone might see how radiant she looked. And the food would be the talk of the town.

'Tomorrow, Simeon,' she said, 'you will come and cook for me as you have never cooked before.'

Simeon cast off his dusty blackness and the cook arose like a phoenix from the ashes.

'Memsahib, I shall do my best.'

At midday Stephanie ate her lunch. The baby awoke early for her one o'clock feed so must wait. Ayah paced up and down with the distraught child over her shoulder.

She looked at Stephanie sitting calmly on the verandah, eating her three-course meal followed by coffee and cheese and biscuits and hated her. Up and down, up and down walked Ayah, checking her watch for the time until the baby was soothed by the rhythm of her movement. The golden head leaned heavy on her shoulder, the tiny body moulded itself to the contour of her breast. Ayah sang in the dappled sunlight and wished that the day would last for ever.

Ursula took Isaac's hand and they wandered through the jungle towards the lake. Isaac paddled in the mud and traced patterns with a long stick in the slime at the water's edge.

Ursula sat and stared into the water, worrying about the future, about how much longer she could enjoy the peace of her home. She even contemplated kidnapping Isaac and fleeing the country as a last resort.

One o'clock. Ayah walked up the verandah steps as the clock struck. She knelt and placed the baby on Memsahib's knee, relieved that at last her baby would be fed.

'Memsahib, please,' Ayah whispered not daring to look up.

'I work for you, I look after baby. You not pay. I not want anything. Please, Memsahib?'

Ayah looked up at the memsahib with her hair a dark halo around her face and wondered that she could have given birth to the child only two days previously.

'Memsahib,' whispered Ayah, 'I have present.' From her apron pocket she drew the tiny white nightdress with embroidered ducks swimming round the yoke and laid it reverently on Memsahib Stephanie's lap.

Stephanie, with the child to her breast, fingered the fine material with her free hand and studied Ursula's fine stitching. She wondered whether Ursula knew the nightdress was missing. Of course, she was unlikely to need it again. Stephanie smiled to think of Ursula's husband's baby wearing it, and only she would know.

'Susan's sister, she wear,' murmured Ayah.

Stephanie flung the garment as far from her as she could.

'How dare you?' she screamed.

'Mummy, I'm cold,' wailed Isaac. Ursula looked up at the sun and realised how long she had been sitting by the lake. She put her arms round Isaac and held him close. When she released him there were muddy fingermarks on her neck and streaks stained the front of her dress but they did not bother her.

'Come,' she said. 'We will go home and have a hot bath and some tea. That will warm you.'

Hand in hand they followed the narrow trail made by their own feet. The grass was high over Isaac's head. From the house only Ursula's head and shoulders could be seen, and the brilliant orange blob that was her sun hat.

Stephanie fed her baby and went to join the rest of the family at the pool.

'I'll be back at five,' she called as the car door slammed.

But the baby had been kept waiting for her feed and crying and had gulped down mouthfuls of air. A pocket of wind seethed and churned the warm pool of milk in her stomach. She drew her legs up to her chest, her fingers clawed at the sheets and she screamed in pain.

Ayah lay the baby on her knee, face down. She gently massaged her back until the wind exploded bringing most of the feed with it. Ayah worried that she would soon be hungry again and there were three and a half hours to go until her mother returned. If only Memsahib had a bottle! Ayah searched the nursery, she asked her friend.

'Memsahib, she say bottle is not good.'

'Why she say that?' wondered Ayah and thought of the misery it could prevent. Perhaps if she were to buy a bottle and some powdered milk and show Memsahib how simple it was? And the baby would not cry.

Ayah wheeled out the pram, the beautiful pram she had polished with her friend. She fetched clean sheets from the nursery. The baby cried when Ayah put her down. Ayah adjusted the sun shade and sang and rocked the pram. She walked down the garden watched by the gardener. Her back was straight and her head held high. For an hour she pushed the pram round the garden ignoring the attempts of the shamba to attract her attention. Then the baby began to stir, snuffling its nose into the sheets, the mouth searching from side to side.

Ayah looked at her watch. Memsahib would not be back for two hours. Ayah felt in her pocket for her purse and headed for the gate.

Isaac fresh from his bath, in clean clothes, carried a basket of bricks onto the verandah steps. The late afternoon sun was pleasantly warm on his back and the concrete reflected its softening glow. He built a castle. Turrets and domes, battlements and ramparts. He had never seen such a marvel but his mummy had told him about the knights on horseback who wore silver armour.

The outer wall was complete but the inner wall required more height and the bricks were running short. One way round his predicament would be to build the central tower on a higher step. He moved forward, then stopped with a cry of rage and disappointment for a snake lay in the way.

'Go away,' he shouted, waving his arms. The snake did not move.

'Mummy,' yelled Isaac. 'Mummy, there's a snake in my way.'

'Oh yes, dear,' Ursula was writing a letter.

'Mummy, the snake is spoiling my game.'

Ursula thought that perhaps she could use the farm as a bargaining point. Surely money or land could settle anything, even a question of adoption.

'Mummy, please come.'

'Whatever is it, Isaac? Can't you see I'm busy?'

'But Mummy, I can't be busy because of the snake.'

Ursula threw down her writing pad and stomped to the top of the verandah steps.

'Oh God,' she said.

Ayah reached the shopping centre and parked the pram outside the chemist. She picked up the baby, her string bag and purse, and went inside. She bought sterilising tablets, a bottle and teat and a tin of milk powder.

'Gold Cap please,' she said. Memsahib had always insisted on Gold Cap. She said it was the best.

Outside Ayah juggled with her bag and covered the baby's head with a shawl to keep off the sun. She walked straight past the shiny pram and in the direction of the bus stop.

The snake which had slept in the sun while Isaac played, was awakened by the vibrations of Ursula's tread. The reptilian head reared and looked at her over the top step, tongue flickering. Ursula stood still, her hands clasped to her cheeks.

'Isaac, go and find Shamba. Tell him to come and kill the snake.'

'No, Mummy, you shouldn't hurt him.' Isaac leaned closer and closer. 'Look, Mummy, he's lovely. All green and yellow.' Ursula's heart almost stopped beating. The curly lashes and the large eyes were so close, so vulnerable and she couldn't protect him.

'Isaac, will you do as I tell you. Go and find Shamba.' If she turned and went through the house to the front door, she feared Isaac might follow.

'What a lovely snake,' said Isaac. 'Can I stroke it, Mummy?'

Ayah walked briskly home from the bus stop and unlocked her front door. She laid the baby on the bed, wedged in with pillows. Memsahib said that was important, you could never tell when the baby might manage to roll over and fall off. It was a good habit to get into.

Ayah took the vase from the window sill and dropped the plastic roses into the rubbish bin. She filled the vase with water and added one sterilising tablet. The tablet bubbled and vanished just as she had remembered.

While the bottle and teat soaked she ran to the bathroom for more water, locking and unlocking the door as she left and returned. Susan always had a bath before her five o'clock feed. Ayah scrubbed the washing-up bowl until her wrists ached. She could see no sign of germs.

She filled the bowl and tested the water temperature with her elbow. She added a dash more hot and a drop more cold and it was just right.

The kettle boiled again for the feed, and stood cooling while Ayah struggled through the jungle of poppers on the ill-fitting baby-gro. She smiled to see the baby stiffen then relax in the warm water. She was as white as in her dreams, with Bwana's long fingers and Memsahib Stephanie's ears as dainty as sea shells. Then Ayah dressed the baby in the delicate nightgown and tested the heat of the bottle on the inside of her wrist.

Ursula wondered whether she could jump over the snake. She lifted the long skirts of her caftan. At the sudden movement the snake lifted its head and raised its hood, like a poke bonnet. Ursula stepped slowly and quietly towards the back of the verandah.

'Two meters.' She calculated and drew an imaginary circle around the snake. As she moved backwards, Isaac moved forwards. She tried to recall everything she had ever read about the spitting cobra. The eyes must not be rubbed, she remembered, but washed out with milk. But was there any milk left? Would it be enough? She thought of the small jug on the breakfast table.

'Isaac,' called his mother. 'Go back down the steps into the garden. Walk round to the servants quarters and see if any one is there.'

'No. The prickles will hurt my feet.'

Ursula thought of the days when Isaac would have walked barefoot over any surface.

'Charity!' shrieked Ursula. 'Shamba!'

Isaac stood still, halted by the fear in her voice. Ursula's voice echoed back, trapped in the heavy layers of greenery engulfing the verandah.

Only Charity's daughter was anywhere near, blowing the charcoal to prepare an evening meal for Charity and Shamba in the weed-strewn yard and she was hard of hearing. Charity and Shamba were far away in Memsahib's vegetable garden hoeing between the tall rows of maize.

Isaac was alarmed by Ursula's fear and felt his own danger.

'Mummy, cuddle me,' he whimpered. He stretched his arms towards her and stumbled through the ruins of his castle.

'What you doing?' asked Simeon as he clattered through the door.

Ayah cradled the baby in her arms and ran her fingers through the soft hair. Tomorrow she would buy powder and a soft pink brush.

'You mad?' inquired Simeon.

'What you doing, woman?' He walked up to Ayah and shook her shoulder, trying to get some response.

'That Memsahib Stephanie's baby?' Simeon paced up and down brandishing a newspaper. Ayah hummed softly without looking up.

'I go,' said Simeon. He pulled one of Ayah's suitcases from under the bed and began throwing things into it as fast as he could. Bwana's old clothes. Recipe books. Memsahib's jars of spices. A coffee pot.

'You mad, woman? The police come put you in prison.'

Simeon stripped the blankets from the bed and rolled them into a bundle. He saw the collapse of his dreams. There would be no cooking at Memsahib Stephanie's; no more mousses and sponges and fillet steaks en croûte.

'You not see me again,' he screamed, pale with fear under the black skin.

Isaac screamed until Ursula longed for him to stop. She pinned his arms to his sides and imprisoned his hands with her own.

'Stop that noise, Isaac. Speak to me.' She fought to manoeuvre the kicking four-year-old through to the kitchen. She lay him on the cold floor and poured the clotted remains from the small milk jug over his eyes, then jug after jug of water. Isaac choked and spluttered and fought even harder as the water poured into his mouth and ears and streamed onto the floor.

Still he screamed and the sound pounded in her head, swamping all thought until she felt she would drown in its waves. If only he would stop.

The doctor, she thought. She must ring for the doctor. But she could not manage the phone and the screaming child. If she released his hands he might rub his eyes and endanger his sight. First she had to quieten the child, then she would be able to get to the phone.

In the small white room she laid Isaac on the bed, with her body on top of his to hold him down. She felt each breath's gasping inflow and waited for its expulsion in a scream of agony.

'Hush, Isaac, hush. I'm here. Mummy's here.' She tried to stroke his head but he was tossing violently from side to side. He would not let her help him. Yet she was holding him for his own good, because she loved him. But that noise, the sound of his pain was killing her. She had to stop it.

With one hand Ursula pulled the pillow from under Isaac's

head. He bit her arm and she knew that she could not hold him for much longer.

She just wanted to cover his head with the pillow to deaden the noise for long enough to think – until he was quiet and she could bathe his eyes and ring for the doctor. As soon as the screams were muffled she felt relieved.

She could cope now. She felt calmer. She began to sing the song she had sung to him so often as a baby. Brahms' lullaby brought peace to them both. Isaac's legs stopped thrashing, the rasping panic went out of his breathing and Ursula's heart stopped pounding. She put her ear to the pillow and was reassured by the silence.

Ursula stood up and replaced the pillow beneath Isaac's head. She sang quietly, so as to comfort but not disturb him. She fetched a bowl of water and gently mopped the swollen eyes. Isaac would feel better after a good sleep. She straightened the distorted limbs and gently tucked in the blankets and bedspread.

'There's my baby,' she murmured. Ursula tiptoed towards the door and vowed that if anything happened to Isaac's eyes, she would be his sight. She would dedicate her life to him. He would experience everything through her.

Ursula picked up the phone and dialled the doctor's number.

As Simeon reached the corner of the street a police car turned into the road. The siren wailed and the blue light flashed. Simeon dropped his suitcase and bedroll and ran.

Ayah sat in her room. A shaft of golden sunlight pierced the straggling bushes to dance its dusty blessing over woman and child. A baby's feeding bottle stood empty on the window sill. The woman swayed gently from side to side, dark and strong, crooning a two-tone lullaby.

'Lul-la, baby la.'